Gold Man
Review

Gold Man Review is published once a year by Gold Man Publishing in Salem, Oregon.

The editors invite submissions of previously unpublished works of fiction, nonfiction, and poetry. Manuscripts can be submitted at www.goldmanpublishing.com by following our submission guidelines.

Contents

Letter from the Editors

We can't believe it has already been five years since Gold Man Review was born. When we started Issue 1, we weren't thinking about where we'd be in the future—only that we wanted to be an outlet for work that hadn't an outlet and put authors and poets into print who hadn't had the chance before. Since then, we've had the opportunity to publish award-winning authors, seasoned writers, and even the poet laureate of Oregon, but we've also had the pleasure to publish brand new voices and then watch those authors grow and develop their writing careers.

We've come a long way since that first issue. Five years in and we're still growing. Although the direction of Gold Man is always changing, our dedication to it has not changed and we rely so much on our talented contributors that have supported us through the years, especially as we have gone through several transitions both personal and professional. This year we grew in our reach, pulling in submissions from California, Washington, Alaska, and Hawaii, as well as our native Oregon. We also grew in size, as we had so many high-quality submissions that we ended up with one of our biggest issues yet.

Fittingly, this issue reflects a lot of that growth by opening us up to new worlds and new ways of thinking that can't help but shape us as we read. A few examples of what we have in this year's issue are such pieces as Sarah Isto's "Mourning Hiatus - 5:30 am," Jessica Danger's "Cherry Red Dress," Dorothy Place's "Missing in Action," and Shaun McMichael's "Coming or Going" where we live through the mind-altering messiness of divorce, addiction, and bereavement. In other stories and poems like Kori Rosset's "The Tube Time Slumber Party," Graham Guest's "Blackcorn, Storyteller," and Alex Vigue's "2)," we grow by learning to appreciate a new style or how to peek through a curtain of irony.

We hope that you, too, find something in this issue that helps you grow as a reader, a writer, or as a person.

Thank you for reading.

Editor-in-Chief
Heather Cuthbertson

Managing Editor
Darren Howard

Project Editor
Nicklas Roetto

Executive Editor
Marilyn Ebbs

Associate Editor
Michelle Modesto

Coming or Going

Shaun McMichael

Tonight, Jerome plans on adding six more tallboys of malt liquor to the trail of empty aluminum cans that runs beneath the trees. The trail of cans parallels a major bike path and he plans on adding to the wonder of the normies that will bike by tomorrow in herds with their tight spandex skin. They probably don't wonder why someone might drink there. Even a normie could probably guess that a patch beneath a row of thick juniper would be a nice enough place to pass out. What they probably wonder is why someone would drink like that at all.

Every time he hears a dog bark, he takes a drink. That's his reason tonight.

He started drinking to sirens but something was going down earlier and going by that marker, he would have been empty around 2am and the hours between that emptiness and sunrise would have formed a tunnel from which he might never have emerged.

So now, while drinking to the dogs, he plays another game with the sirens. An old game. When he hears one, he tries to guess, are they coming or going?

A dog barks. He takes a drink. Slows himself. Turns it into a sip. He's got all night and there are a lot of strays in the city. He's heard of packs of them moving together somewhere along the train tracks, maybe by where the canal widens into the bay.

The moon trickles through the needle-cover and falls on his ruddy face. The light is a smooth, methadone mellow. He wonders if the smell of the dusty little pines takes away the smell of himself, a smell he can't smell but can guess by the way the normies slowly tuck their noses into their scarves as if he was a tipped over honey bucket and how they walk around him as if he were leaking out something that could get on their boots.

The sirens at first seemed funny. Like a pack of circus clowns. But he kept hearing them and he's hearing them still, echoing out from the hills, skipping across the bike path and pitching into his squat. What happened? Who bit the big one? What kind of mess will they leave in the morning? For that many sirens, there'll have to be something left to clean up, you'd think.

But are they coming or going? He used to be able to tell. It's in the speed; he used to tell her. Listen! Can you count the seconds before it fades? If more than a dozen, then they were going out to a call. If less, then it's because they know the way, which means they're headed back to Harborview with a live one in the back.

He used to have a police scanner. It sat on the windowsill of the little room they'd given them. When he couldn't sleep, he'd listen to it. She never understood it. Hadn't he had enough sleepless nights? But the more he heard, the less he wanted to join the fun. When you did that, so often you became the center the sirens were rushing toward. They didn't have cable or anything else and they both agreed that the scanner distracted from the cravings until 8am when the clinic opened and they'd go and get their juice anyway. So they'd play coming or going until then.

Another dog barks. Howls. Some big bastard. Close this time. He takes another sip.

He cracks open another. Three left. He can make this. Easy. The corner store that takes his food stamps opens at seven in the a.m. He's pretty sure he can make that. Though you wonder, after sitting through so many tar-headed nights, which one will finally open its mouth wide and leave nothing left of you for the morning to find?

But maybe he can't wait that long. He thinks the closest he could get to death would be riding rails. But he doubts he could throw himself up on an iron horse again. All that's done. That kind of thing takes ambition. Same goes for suicide.

Another siren. The old game. But then there's that deeper question that bites at him now and again. Who are the sirens ringing for? A tweaker taking a crow bar to a K-mart clerk? A cop knocking on the wrong motel door?

They'd play that game too, she and him.

"Coming or going?" she'd ask, a little bored.

"Listen to it! It's got to be coming. Hear how fast that thing just cruised by? Had to only be five, six seconds. Must be an O.D. Yeah. Scored some of the big bad black."

"Think he's going to make it?" she'd ask.

"Why would they keep the siren on otherwise? He'll make it. Just some dipshit doing it alone with no narc-on."

"They run code sometimes even when they're dead," she told him once.

"Just for shits and giggles?"

"So they can get back and go out to lunch," she finished.

So they'd play with a third category. Coming, going or out to lunch. Until she stopped wanting to play anything and started wanting to go out and run around. She started talking about going back to it, the black.

Now there are two howls. The sounds blur with the wails of the ambulances in the hills. He takes two sips. Then a couple more.

Who was the siren for? An old man whose heart just went out? A young kid cutting himself up? A couple on the mend bent back to a bad habit, it ending with the woman dead and the man kicked out again?

He never heard the siren that came for her. They might not have even run code with everything done the way it was. You think there'd have been signs the next morning after something like that but there weren't. No body-chalk, no crimson splotches, no caution tape. The next morning after finding her, he walked away from what had been home and on his way he saw a sparrow bathing in a pothole in the middle of the street. That's all he can remember being different about that morning. That and her blue face, eyes half open below her beanie, dyed yellow hair running out like a stain on the thin carpet. A pant leg rolled up with the needle stuck in.

He doesn't even know how long ago that was now. A day, a year, a decade, last night.

There's a sinking feeling inside. There will be little to show for *this* night. Only another empty can without face or memory in a line of such cans. A line that one could follow to a final squat, waiting out there maybe where the tracks meet the bay where the dogs crawl up from.

He hears the sounds of fur slipping through the trees like hands into wool. He looks up and there are two of them standing before him panting. They're looking at the drops of moonshine glinting through the branches onto his palms. Their spit will be hot on his skin. There's another siren. Coming, going? With this one, he's pretty sure. He pours the rest of the warm liquid out onto his hands and holds out his fingers, shaking. They drink from him and he is gone.

Shaun McMichael

Exegete Nation

Thomas Walton

I can tell that guy across the street
with his cigarette and his curls
is wondering where he should go
not realizing he's already there ... these people!
with their high backs and curved discussions
since when did we all become so skilled
at exegesis? you can't do anything these days
without being explicated, and,
what's worse, when the reflection pool
in the park fills with ducks
some smart-ass comes along
to tell you they're geese!
what are they teaching these kids?
the contents of an organ, for example
aren't the organs the contents?
these gradations, this resistance
to objective truth
has become objective truth
the old rowboat tied to the dock
beneath the willows, let's just
get in it, untie it, row out
and float, just float in the sun
in the sun, in the sun you fucker.

Cherry Red Dress

Jessica Danger

I wore a red satin dress the color of cherry jam, cut differently from the others at the top, because I was the maid of honor. The bride, Jennifer, wore a gown so smothered in tightly woven beadwork you could hear the beads creaking when she walked. After the ceremony, we would set the train into an elegant bustle. The meticulous button and loop system was daunting but Jennifer looked so happy in that dressing room when we saw it done up the first time. She wanted that damn bustle.

The wedding reception was being held in the same hall where, at the age of 10, I had once performed a piano recital. That day, I had worn a pastel dress with obnoxiously poofy sleeves and a tight midsection. My tights were thick, the color of porcelain, and when I sat down I could feel the cool piano bench against the sweaty backs of my knees. My cheap shoes were pinching across the widest part of my foot. I reminded myself to sit up straight by imagining my instructor holding her hand to the small of my back. I told myself again that I could take the shoes off when I was finished. My mother had promised.

The day of the recital a white Steinway baby grand was centered on the stage, a beacon in that giant hall with wood beams above me. My family was in the audience, my mother and father sitting together, trying desperately to get along for the one hour required of them. And my Nana, my maternal grandmother, was always there when it came to piano. She had paid for my piano lessons for years, even paying monthly rental fees for an upright in her library. That was how I knew she took me seriously; she moved out her Stephen King and Dean Koontz novels to make room for the rented piano. She let me in there after school, for as long as I wanted, to play the piano or read away from all the other kids she babysat, in the quiet cool back room full of books and music and macramé. At the recital she sat front and center, fanning her face with the program, wearing too much jewelry and too much White Diamond perfume, smiling at me with all that bright lipstick, her favorite shade, Chanel's "Inspiration."

But that was 11 years ago. The baby grand was pushed off to the side of the stage and hidden under a cover. I waited outside for Jennifer and her new husband, Tim, to arrive in the limo. My tote bag sagged with her bouquet and her extra shoes and I really wanted a glass, many glasses, of her champagne. It was hot that May and I could feel the makeup sliding down my face, my scalp baking under the tangle of hairsprayed curls. I wanted a cigarette and reached into my purse for one. I saw that I had missed fourteen calls from my brother, Jon.

I'd been looking forward to this day for months: I had a babysitter for my five-year-old son. Time to myself; time to enjoy with friends. But I was also a woman who had entered motherhood in her teens, and alone, and my entire body was attuned to danger. Listening to my brother's voice coming through my cell phone, my hands were shaking although I didn't know it until I dropped my cigarette into the yards of cheap red satin that billowed around my waist.

Dad had been walking around the side of the house, my brother said. No one knew where he was going, or why. He made it around the corner, closest to the garage, and, sidling between the boat trailer and the wall, he had a grand mal seizure. He hadn't drunk enough that day. Was trying to get through this one Saturday with just Budweiser instead of the hard stuff, the vodka or gin that really got him going in the morning. Instead, he'd had only beer, *Just some Buds*, he'd told himself. It wasn't enough and his body let him know that. He slumped, collapsing onto the concrete and, his body twisting, began to seize uncontrollably. It was the softened sound of his skull repeatedly hitting the stuccoed concrete wall that eventually alerted a neighbor, several minutes later. The fire department recognized the address, but it still took the ambulance nine minutes to arrive.

Jenn and Tim's limo pulled up and Tim got out first. I could see them from where I stood on the sidewalk, down the block a bit, in the shade. I told my brother I would meet him at the county hospital. I watched Jenn get out of the limo. Her pearl tipped hairpins caught the sun as she turned her head, her eyes squinty as she scanned the crowd for me, the best friend who was supposed to be right there when she got out, returning her bouquet, helping her unfurl her train. I sneaked out the back door, grazing that creamy baby grand on my way out. I wanted to sit down on that bench. I wanted to play it like I did when I was a child, fearless, my eyes closed and back straight, with a whole family in the audience, and my grandmother beaming at me in all her gaudy glory. I wanted to take a bow again at the end. *Never a curtsy*, I told my instructor. I would never curtsy.

On my way out, after handing over her bouquet and telling her mother I had to go, I looked at Jenn. I couldn't dare tell her that I was leaving. She stood up for her first dance. Her husband took her hand, leading her out onto the dance floor. Her train was dirty. No one had bustled her up.

The hospital waiting room was full. My brother, Jon, was seated on an aisle chair, his body turned as far away from the masses as possible. Only 13 months younger than me, he looked like my father. That strong square chin, the wrinkles at the corner of his eyes. His hands were clenched together and even from the doorway I could tell that he had been grinding his molars. He bounced his left leg up and down. Jon hated conflict, crowds, and strangers. I walked toward him and hugged him. He stood out of his chair and made like he had stretched.

"Jess. I gotta get out of here. I can't fucking do this." Stunned, I watched my brother walk out of the waiting room, his shoulders square and broad, fists balled and shoved deep into his pockets. This was not the first time I had watched him walk away from me. I was 16, he was 15, and we were driving to school one morning. We were arguing in traffic at the intersection of Pacific Coast Highway and Crenshaw Boulevard in front of the shopping center where we used to while away summer days. Jon simply opened his door, got out of my idling Chevelle and walked across three lanes of traffic, toward the sidewalk holding his skateboard. I drove to school and called our mother at work. He didn't come home that night, or the night after. My mother would wait up nights for him, smoking her long white cigarettes in the kitchen window.

I took my shoes off and stood there in the waiting room, in line with all these other people, still wearing thigh-high pantyhose and a bridesmaid's dress, waiting to tell the woman behind the bulletproof glass at the registration desk, the one that wouldn't even make eye contact with me, that I was there to claim my father.

My father did try to get sober a few times. I would take him to rehab, unlatching my son's car seat so that Dad could recline in the back on the drive to the hospital to de-tox. I would sit in on his family counseling sessions and let him tell me why it was all my fault, that I was just like my mother, "that bitch." Then he would relapse, sometimes living on the street before coming back to the dilapidated home his grandparents had left him. After years of trying to parent my father and my son, I had stopped. I told my father I loved him and I drove away in my green pick-up, the truck he used to help me repair when I couldn't afford a mechanic. It was like a divorce.

The hallway was quiet. I held my high heels in one hand and pinned my visitor's badge to the top of my dress, catching the top of the strapless push up bra that I was dying to take off. It felt like it took forever to finally find the door to my father's room. The hallway seemed ridiculously long, like the walk to confession on Friday nights, where you just stare forward and keep moving your feet. At the end of the hall, just inside the door, was my father with that familiar stale cigarette smell. It used to be Benson & Hedges, then Marlboro Light's, then the divorce, then Dad switched to Parliaments when he had extra money from recycling, then butts from the mall trash cans when he didn't.

Everything was white. His sheets were white, his pillow was white, the curtain separating him from all the other humans moaning and crying in pain around him was white. Three beds down, a round Hispanic woman sat straight up. She stared at me. Her eyes were the color of dark molasses.

I hadn't seen Dad in months. My father's face was puffy, like a marshmallow the moment it hits an open flame, and his right eye so blackened and swollen you couldn't tell it was a lively arctic blue eye that bounced when he laughed at something stupid you said. Or welled up when you told him you loved him. Or gleamed when he called you his Princess or his Sweetie #1. Two weeks earlier, Jon had been called to fish our father out of a gutter in front of a Moose Lodge. Dad was battered and bruised after fighting with a stranger at the bar. He was still recovering from those injuries, and looking at him then had turned my stomach. I didn't want to go any further. I stood there, in my red dress with the cigarette burn, flowers in my hair, wearing fake pearls around my neck, holding my shoes. I hugged my arm tight to my waist, trying to hold onto myself.

I felt guilty just being there.

"Dad?" A whisper, really. I was afraid that he would answer me. I would do this again later, too, when he was lying like this in hospice. I would whisper his name when I got there, praying he wouldn't hear me, so I could leave and then say later, "Well I came but you were sleeping." Like it was his fault. Like it was shameful to be sleeping when you were about to die.

I leaned in closer, holding my shoes to my chest. "Dad. Can you hear me?" He was so thin, wearing only his boxers. They were threadbare and filthy, and I could see right through them. The white hospital sheet was hiding underneath a pilled and filthy oyster-colored blanket tangled at his feet. His knees were knocking together. I tried to soothe him. I rubbed his scrawny little arms and shushed him like I did when my son had a bad dream. I put my high heels down on the plastic hospital chair at the head of his bed.

"It is going to be all right, Dad."

Blue veins and the pale, egg-yolk yellow of his jaundiced skin. I tried to loosen his fingers, but couldn't. Instead, he gripped harder.

"Dad ... shhh ..." I took each finger, one-by-one until he relaxed his hold. I worked around his knuckles, those busted up knobby mountains of flesh. I was careful to work around the blood that had congealed in the cracks of his fingernails. I rolled him over, just a little bit, too frightened at the prominence of his hipbones to do anything significant. I pulled the blanket up from his skinny ankles and tucked him in. I didn't want to touch him, not really, but I did pet his head and straighten his hair. There was something stuck in it. Later I learned it was matted blood, so clumped from the days in that hospital bed that I had to cut it all out. He refused a real hair cut, so for months he walked around with half a head of hair.

My father continued to seize throughout the night. I watched as long as I could. It was too quiet and that woman in the next bed stared at me with those big molasses eyes. I left him there, walked back out into the hall, leaving my shoes on the chair beside him. They didn't matter; they were dyed to match that cherry jam dress. There I was, walking down that impossibly long hallway again, a woman that just had to identify her father in a sea of hospital beds with a cigarette burn in her dress, no shoes on her feet.

Elegy for Old Friend Iain

Lillo Way

Just as water arced between hose bib and grass blade
       at the moment car tires crunched the driveway gravel
and our neighbor's phone rang inside the summer window
       where a flapping gauze curtain almost caught a sparrow
who was in the midst of calling *Three Three Three Three*
       while a float plane scooped down to the lake
drowning out the hedge-clipper below and the siren beyond
       when inside the house the blades of the bedroom fan
began to turn slowly in reverse and I was humming
       How are Things in Glocca Morra as I lifted
the clean white-load from the washer into the dryer
       exactly at that instant you left the body
and your throat rattled goodbye.

Beer is for Beasties

Travis Laurence Naught

Most people don't drink so much in the bathroom. Of course, most people don't see monsters every time they look out the window. The bathroom doesn't have any windows. Jim Sheridan sits in his Dive Lodge rental bathroom most every night since his divorce. The outside world offers horror in place of splendor.

He carries different types of booze with him depending on what he's been seeing recently: whiskey is for werewolves; gin, ghosts; Zinfandel, zombies. Just kidding on that last one. There's no such thing as zombies. But the others are oh so true, and this is just the tip of the iceberg when it comes to Jimmy's drinking rules.

It all started during the divorce proceedings. Madeline was sitting across the table with her high-priced lawyer. Jim should have asked her to keep both hands where he could see them, please, but it was too late for that. Behind his soon-to-be ex-wife and her philandering representation, a window with a view across the alley put on quite a show. Every rebuttal to Jim's lawyer's arguments for receiving alimony was played out through the glass like a gruesome game of hangman.

"You willingly gave her the money." Mr. Fancypants graduated top of his class from Gonzaga Law. Such a fine education was overkill for keeping poor Jim's backside in its proverbial sling. "That little envelope you gave my client the money in, the one on which you clearly printed: I WON'T EVEN HOLD YOU RESPONSIBLE IF YOU LOSE IT, exonerates Maddie of any fiscal recompense to which you may feel entitled."

As the nails were steadily hammered into his monetary coffin lid, hope for a taste of his wife's profits made from his seed money being sealed off forever, an apparition was visible in the other office setting up a chair. Jim stopped paying any attention to the jargon when the apparition climbed on top of the chair and started flipping its necktie toward the ceiling fan above him like a rope. It looked like an active suicide attempt in progress.

"Call 911! He's trying to kill himself!" Knowing what he does now, he would've simply taken a sip of a stiff drink to banish the vision. Alcohol was for apparitions.

Everyone in the office followed Jim's arm with his or her eyes to look at whatever he was pointing toward. Madeline let out a contemptuous snort upon finding no more than an empty room for her troubles turning around. While Jim's legal representative was no Mr. Fancypants, she knew the only way she would be getting paid was to win her client a settlement. Lilly Newsome recognized her opportunity to strike and took it.

"My client is threatening self-harm. I move for a one percent allotment of profits earned during Madeline and Jim's union to assuage his psychological trauma. Besides, Fancypants, I'm sure it wouldn't be difficult to prove recent extramarital affairs and aim at a higher percentage."

Jim never wanted more than his original $10,000 back. He would have objected to the obscene amount of money agreed on if he had been aware of what was going on around him. As it was though, the first occurrence of his visions grossed a tidy $219,000 for his having posted the start up money to Madeline's wildly successful psychic phone line service: **Read It or Weep**.

Lilly Newsome ended up with $75,000 for her efforts. Dealing with suicidal clients could create unsettling case histories, and she cajoled poor Jim into steep compensation. He agreed, not wanting to be dragged through another legal proceeding. She threatened coercion of her talents, founded in doubts that he was actually threatening suicide.

"No reason I can't take you out for drinks with some of your newfound money though." Lilly was actually hitting on him. It felt like an internet troll comment on his love life. Unfortunately, nobody was around to offer Jim a shot of troll-chasing tequila, so he just had to politely decline. "FINE," she belched back at him. Her skin visibly began to droop, changing colors, and she grew a tail while walking away.

Several other unfortunate visions began dancing in front of Jim's eyes over the next 24 hours. It was as if severing the marital bond with his now famous ex-wife came with consequences for which he was ill prepared. As if in response to this thought, Jim's phone rang. The voice on the other end cryptically recited the following poem:

> "Whenever by creepies you're feeling confounded,
>   or haunted by spirits that make you feel hounded,
> drinking's the answer to dull their effects;
>   beer is for beasties, you'll learn of the rest."
>   *CLICK!*

The off-the-hook alarm reminded Jim to hang up the phone twenty seconds later. He decided to check the caller ID after composing himself. Lo and behold, the number revealed itself as coming from Madeline's city-sized number exchange. She must have found out where he was staying after she kicked him out, after he caught her cheating. To heck with the legal system, it was time for Jim to take matters into his own hands.

All of the calls were set to dial into the same switchboard before connecting to any one of four thousand "certified professionals" just waiting for your call. More like certifiable. Returning the call of a specific employee, especially without even a fake first name, would seem to be impossible. Jim set to dialing the same number over and over again. With a $9.99 connection fee at each dial, plus a twenty-minute minimum conversation at $4.99 per minute, the charges turned into a mathematical vampire. Twenty-eight days later, thank God for a phone cord that reached both the restroom and refrigerator/microwave combo in his hotel room, because after a total of 1,990 unsuccessful attempts, a familiar voice spoke another set of rhyming phrases into his ear:

> "You've gotten to the bottom of her little scheme,
> but the total of charges will not leave you pleased;
> they equal awards given you in the settlement.
> Crack open some vodka, forget for your betterment."
> *CLICK!*

Ullage was easier to drink on encountering a unicorn than filling the emptiness Jim felt at that moment. That was when the drinking started. He emptied the limited, four double-shot bottles provided by Dry Fly Distillery. Mixing the bourbon, whiskey, and gin did nothing for the sting of having his newfound money bled from his account, but as soon as the vodka went down, life got better. Vodka was for vampires. Jim figured out that the rules, in fact, helped more than he originally assumed they would.

Mr. Fancypants had agreed to meet him for the legal transfer of funds on the same night as a full moon. He could swing by the Dive Lodge with a check on his way home from the office. It would be nearly six o'clock in the evening. The sun went down at 4:15 p.m. An unexpected sight for Jim was casting a rather mundane shadow for everyone else, considering the girth and drool dripping sounds he encountered on opening the door.

"Hello, Mr. Sheridan." The voice was right, but it was emitted from the snarling mouth of what looked like a Stephen King monster. "I've got your check and require a signature of receipt." His claws forwarded a piece of paper that somehow was not shredded.

Jim dove for the bathroom and locked himself in. "Slide it under the door!"

Travis Laurence Naught

He picked himself up off the floor moments later and started unscrewing the cap on the bottle of mouth rinse. Whiskey would have been best, sure, but anything to abolish memories of such a horrifying vision would have to work in this pinch. A paper slid into the room about the time he got three gulps down. *I'll Be Right Back* was written rather neatly across an envelope.

Two more gulps and the quiet coming from the other side of the bathroom door helped calm Jim's nerves. His plan was to be just drunk enough from peppermint-y breath freshener to deal with Fancypants when he returned. He was trying to compose himself before the wereman got back.

Looking in the mirror at himself was quite the shock. Wild facial hair and a crop of acne were the defining features covering his once rugged face. A quick sniff test proved that his breath was even more offensive, regardless of the recently swallowed product. He was still wearing the same suit from his divorce hearing nearly a month ago. It did not matter that Jim used the toilet on a regular basis while on the phone, his clothes were filthy for having not been changed.

He took another look at the twenty-ounce bottle that was nearly half gone. Fancypants had somehow transformed into one of the scariest images he'd ever seen. Emptying the bottle down his gullet would surely make the next interaction easier. Jim gritted his teeth and began guzzling the rest of the forty-five proof blue liquid. Maybe it was too much, or a combination of bodily stressors, but the poor man passed out before he finished.

A ringing telephone woke Jim up. He started to crack his eyes open, but blinding white surroundings forced him to shut them again. Things were soft to the touch. He realized this quickly as he started to roll over for the noise. Jim could not remember where he was. All he really knew was that whatever his wife had made for dinner last night gave him some pretty outstanding nightmares. Going to have to ask Madeline to expunge whatever it was from the recipe catalogue. Someone else finally picked up the receiver and the one-sided conversation sounded a little something like this:

"Eastern State Hospital ... Yes, he still appears catatonic ...
    Schizophrenic, paranoid; acted on his suicidal tendencies ...
Doctors think a shot could make the poor man panic,
        but maybe when he wakes, if his mind's ill at ease."
            CLICK!

2)

Alex Vigue

"write more than just repeating his favorite songs' lyrics"
  – Amber Tamblyn

I am the glass table that has been jumped on by the family dog.
                    Shattered, swollen, apart.

I am the coffee table in the wine bar willed with old corks
                    daughter of winos
                    son of corkscrews

I am the armless red chair
pinned into itself
reupholstered enough times that I am plumper

I am the manual clock that must be changed for daylight savings
                    I can't change my own face
                    but it feels right half of the time.

The Annunciation of Charles Nightcloud

J.L. Cooper

A checkered-shirted, pockmarked angel of a trucker dropped me off ten miles outside of Socorro, New Mexico, back when I was open-ended, hitchhiking, preferring a freezing night in the high desert to an indifferent girl in Albuquerque. I walked a little further under soft white clouds. When they vanished in a moonless night, I named emerging stars. The first was Panacea, then her sister, Mirage, and cousin Sofia, which created a triangle in the southern sky with Silhouette and the red star, Mercy.

Frost framed my wool cap while thousands of stars brought certainty to my smallness. I hoped for invisibility in my sleeping bag, but a pack of coyotes caught my scent. I was a green city kid with a wild imagination, shuddering at their yelps, imagining the alpha coyote taking a lunge at my leg. The coyotes animated, making sounds too close to frenzy. I breathed again when a closer yelp quieted the pack with a definitive call. The quiet screamed back that I was a shallow breath, nothing more than the click of a breaking twig.

I remember morning. Delirium was the price for its arrival. I shook off visions of a desert death like I used to shake water from my hair after a predawn swim. When the sun cracked the desert open, it gave birth to small stark shadows. I sat on the edge of the empty road; nothing came for hours. I tossed pebbles to the pavement. Before they bounced and settled, I tried to predict the side that would face the sky, and see if being right made a difference.

I was just short of naming my favorite rocks when a man walked right out of the sagebrush. "I'm Charlie," he said, as if I'd known him in another form and needed a little hint. He'd been out there all night too. "Bitch of a night," he said, this being the first frost of the year, and he ought to know, telling me he was native to these parts and used another language when he talked to coyotes.

He was the one who called the pack away from us last night. Charlie said talking to animals came easy. His real trouble was telling his wife about the bothering. He couldn't name it otherwise, but admitted she deserved to know when he was troubled and needed to come out here.

"Shall I call you Charlie?"

"Well, I'm Charlie to everyone who knows me; Sagebrush Charlie to some. I was named after my father, a man passing through. His name was Charles. Nobody knew him much, especially my mother. She taught me to talk to animals."

He looked over my shoulder, but his eyes didn't focus anywhere.

"I don't know why she gave me his name. She must have seen something in him worth looking at in me. I tried asking her when she was dying, and I try asking her now, but the wind changes direction every time I think I hear her answering."

He told me he was acquainted with ditches, and said it in a noble way, like he was offering wisdom to a loved one. His habit was to stand in the road and put a thumb in the direction the next car or truck was headed.

"It doesn't matter where they're headed, since I always come back here," he said. He never ventured more than a hundred miles before turning back. He talked to men, always men, about anything they wanted to say—like where they wanted to go if they live long enough to retire, if they were in some pain, or what they hoped to leave or find.

Soon enough, they'd show him if they preferred conversation, the radio, or the wind coming through the open window. He was more at ease with wind because he likened it to a dream. Sometimes, he'd simply say, "That's far enough for me," to summarize the day. His black hair seemed in motion even when the wind abated; it covered half the worry lines in his brow—more like rivers, but not as deep as his desert eyes when they fixed on the sight of me. I was thinking he might be a Sephardic mystic, showing up every hundred years, or just a man overdue for recognition, maybe Sainthood, but he wasn't a man of cloth.

After all, he talked to coyotes, snakes, and birds. He was amiable, with no judgment meant to harm. Wasn't he a variation of St. Francis? He blessed the high desert, said he was close to the source of his bothering, and it scared him less and less. He told me he was forty but knew he looked sixty. He could have been six hundred; I could see the part of him that lived beyond wind and drink.

Charlie turned in a minimal way, and asked me, dead serious, as if we were debating scriptures, what I thought would come upon us next: a pickup truck, a sedan, or an eighteen-wheeler?

For the sake of shadows shortening, I asked, "Are those my only choices?" When I saw he wasn't going to answer, I told him a white pickup will likely come next, with two men going to work.

"Is that all you've got? What else happens?"

I gave the matter my best thought, since Charlie wouldn't budge an inch from serious.

"Ok, here's what happens. One of them had a big fight with his wife the night before and wants to talk about it, but can't find a way to start, so he runs his hand down his leg with tense, uncertain aim, and this gets the attention of the other man, who says, 'hey, I get those cramps too,' but the first man says, 'it's not a cramp, it's something else,' and that starts a conversation about long straight roads in deserts—how hypnotic they are. Each man takes a drink of water, but it doesn't help the other kind of thirst. Neither takes his eyes off the road while talking about their boss, who gives them constant trouble. They don't see the futility of complaining. Then the first man mentions his wife in a lowered tone, as if she's looking at him from the dashboard, trying to believe in him, but he doesn't tell about the argument, not yet, which was bruising and unfinished. He realizes she's been trying to get through to him. The wind coming in the open window flips their empty paper coffee cups around the cab of the truck. As they tumble around, each man offers a list of physical injuries he's endured. Back and forth it goes, for the next thirty miles. The good part is they both recognize a kind of sweetness on the topic of endurance."

Charlie said, "Not bad, I see a lot of that between men. A whole lot of it."

A pause came upon Charlie like a breathless visitation; he even closed his eyes. A pause in the desert is unlike any other, on account of the crusted earth and sand absorbing most of your presence and half your intention. You have to work extra hard to see what's in your mind before claiming it belongs to you, and even then, maybe it doesn't. Charlie was at peace with that kind of uncertainty. It gave him a private smile.

He took a breath and said, "I see them too. Although they don't like their work, they never look for other jobs. When they run dry talking about it, one man says:

'You know, we pass this stretch of road going seventy every single day, and never stop to see what it feels like when we're not headed somewhere.' The other man says, 'Why the hell would you want to stop in the middle of nowhere,' and the first man says, 'I'm not so sure this is nowhere. What if this is where we might find a little peace but we don't stop because we're afraid to be alone and don't even know that silence can be a good thing?' The second man goes him one more, saying, 'What if it's not silence we fear, it's our insignificance?'"

Charlie was so deep in the story, and I the listening, we waited out the sound of a jet overhead because we needed the desert in our minds.

He took a gentle breath.

"Well, the first man gets pissed, saying, 'you're full of shit, go ahead, stop the truck right now and we'll see, I have to piss anyway.' But they end up driving five more miles without either one speaking; each man is trying to figure out what else he means to say. The driver is uneasy, grows into his own resolve, and says, 'Ok, I'm stopping now. I'm going to spend a few minutes standing out here without talking. Nothing personal. You know, you've been my best friend for twenty-seven years, I just did the numbers.'

'What do you mean, the numbers? Of course you're my best friend.'

'I practically had to push you on the dance floor with a bulldozer when you met your wife. That's the serious fear I'm talking about. You took it from there just fine. I want a little credit. You never thanked me for getting you past your fear.'"

Charlie squared himself to me at that juncture and said, "That's it, that's as far as I've gone with the imaginary men. The next part hasn't come to me."

"Wait a minute, does the friend give the credit or not?"

"Well, I don't know, let me think on it." He kicked some rocks around and watched for signs on the horizon. A lizard came and went.

"All right, the truck is slowing down, but it's taking a while, because the driver puts it in neutral and doesn't use the brakes. In the slowing, they start talking about all they've done for each other: loans of fishing rods, building sheds on Sundays, making runs to the feed store when one of them was sick. Their conversation takes on the tone of a deathbed scene. The truck finally stops and the conversation ends. They get out and walk in separate directions. One starts to get some tears, but the other just stares at the ground, thinking there's nothing for him out here, but starts to wonder what makes him so certain."

"Is that all you've got? What happens next? It's just imaginary men you know. You can make anything happen."

"All right, you've got me going. I'm going to say the friend gives credit, they get back in the truck and drive off, and that starts a conversation about looking down a straight road until it narrows to a point and is gone. Some day, I swear, I'm going to make a version where men and roads and trucks aren't even part of the story."

We discussed the matter until the sun began to burn. I was heartened when Charlie agreed our stories had overlapping parts. He said I was dead right about the tense, uncertain aim of the soothing hand. He was less certain about the men never taking their eyes off the road. He thinks their eyes go everywhere, but that was one of the things they weren't ready to know.

I was wrong about the pickup truck coming next. What came was just a little wind kicking up a dust devil. Charlie smiled like a mentor does, telling me he was messing with me a little, and not to worry about being right, since whatever came to mind was worthy of attention.

"I used to worry about who will pick me up, get a little hopeful, but most people pass me like I'm a rock and nothing else. I learned not to worry. It's too confusing."

Since questions were in the air, I asked him why he came out here to do his thinking. I shivered in the asking while he dug his hand into his jacket for something that used to be there. The motion itself was like a ballad, a story hidden in his way of bringing out his empty hand. He used the hand to support his neck and leaned his head as far back as it would go. I thought this was probably the way his mother held him on the first day of his life—to have a good look at him and welcome him to the world. I figured he needed to let his head be cradled in his own hand, to see if this might bring his mother back.

It was my turn to look down, to respect his privacy. He must have sensed my need to look away, but only looked harder into me.

"Where I end up for the night depends on if I have to move on. I don't do so well around people if they talk to me all at once. That's what I like about you. You don't rush me."

He stared over my right shoulder, twenty degrees above the horizon.

"My wife knows when I'm restless, and goes to do some prayer. She puts me to bed just right, better than I can do for myself."

He must have read my next question from my eyes and said her name was Celina. He said it so softly, we saw into her worries like they were hovering above the horizon. I saw where he was looking—saw a shimmering there and he said, "I know," to the shimmering; it made him sad, and I was sad too.

Charlie played with time and fate. He told me his goal was to stay alive until he saw evidence for a life when everybody stopped trying so hard to wreck things. He wanted a world where the important things weren't taken from a man. He's known too many people who didn't say they were dying, but didn't rise from the sagebrush to announce that living was a larger cause.

His food was gone. I pulled a bag of chips from my backpack, but he asked, "Got a cigarette?" I told him no, because I tried smoking but I was a swimmer and it was not worth the loss of breath and coughing all the time. He smiled and said, "It's all right, I go to a place for water too," but he couldn't elaborate because fate was coming in the form of a barreling truck.

Charlie tried to wave the trucker down using both hands in a friendly gesture. The trucker didn't stop, but the wind from the truck lifted the bag of chips right out of my hand, thirty feet up, tracing a perfect arc in the New Mexico morning. The bag drifted down, while we held, for its entire flight, our judgments and sins in abeyance. We came to the moment together. It was the moment between the strike of a match and the lighting of a chapel candle. Our remembrance of last night brought us down to the pavement edge. He lifted his head before I lifted mine, to announce, "I've been waiting for a sign, and now I see two: that truck didn't swerve to hit me, and I didn't jump in front of it like I planned on yesterday."

I was a kid, not an angel or a sage. I told him I was glad on both accounts. I declared him wise, told him I didn't want him to die, that the men in the imaginary pickup truck were on the verge of seeing something incredible, beyond fear, and they'd need him in the desert silence. I told him he had a gift and a sorrow beyond the figuring, and said:

"You can't just leave those guys in the middle of a story. I won't either." I added two more observations, respecting Charlie as the master of signs. "That trucker wasn't the one you need. Plus, I saw your love when you said the word, Celina." I added, "You know, maybe that bag still has some chips in it."

Charlie walked over to the bag like an attorney examining Exhibit A and found my speculation true. We shared what remained in the bag, witnessed by the morning. He spoke to the road itself, the sagebrush, and finally to me, announcing it was time he set out for home.

He didn't use the road, but took sure straight steps across the open land in the direction of Socorro. I yelled to the back of him, "I'm naming a star after you. I'm calling it Nightcloud. It's short for Charles Charlie Nightcloud. You've got more to do here than you know."

I knew he heard me since he raised a stiff right hand while walking away. He held it up there for twenty steps or more, then raised the other hand, laced his fingers to support his tired neck, and kept on walking. He walked that way until I couldn't see him anymore. He didn't turn and he didn't pause, just like a man with special purpose.

the things the world does

Terry Spohn

the world is a tiny radio with one earpiece
it swallows your tongue just when you love it most

it writes the patted book and the man holding the book
and hires the silverfish that feed on the pages

it grows you thin in your long coat and entangles your brow
so that too soon you run free in the family

in the parking lot it's a mantis dining on the death buzz of a locust
the worm in the hull's heart, unseen hand across the prairie grass

and the locust all those years beneath the dirt
the heat close in the cotton of the family

the bone shadows in the shale, cold as
light frozen in a photograph of your father as a child

it's each of the car doors that slam in the sun in the parking lot
and it's almost the time now to say something

with the tongues it has swallowed and the death buzz
beneath the flowers and the bees going backward and forward

outside the dead room and the hearing of nothing inside the dead room
and the face no longer pinched by the bitter odor of day-old coffee

it's your sister between the two silences who says *goodbye Dad*
and the filing out afterward, overdressed, into the afternoon heat

Say Hallelujah

Sandra McDow

"Y'all got any ahra cee Cola?" Rosie's words rolled out in an east
Texas piney-woods drawl. The redhead reached into the oversized,
pink vinyl bag hanging from her right shoulder and fished for change.
"Dang." She removed a Cover Girl makeup compact, tube of strawberry
lip-gloss and miniature canister of L'Oreal hairspray and placed them
on the bar. "Oh, well ... " Rosie retrieved a King James Bible from the
bottom of the bag, flipped it open to Acts, pulled a faded five dollar
bill from between the pages and thrust it toward Scotty. "This ought to
cover it," she said. "And it's lucky ... it's been blessed—it is more blessed
to give than to receive ... Acts 20:35." She gave him a Cheshire cat smile.
"Or maybe it's me been blessed."

Simmons scowled. RC Cola? Bible? She looked more like a sloe-gin
fizz kinda broad. Seated at the corner table at the back of the barroom,
working on a glass of Glen Fiddich on the rocks, he was the club incu-
bus—irascible, ornery and always ready to rumble.

It was his club and his table—and didn't nobody forget that. Mostly
nobody. The last time someone did, a buck sergeant there for the first
time, new stripe making him feel studly, Simmons clarified it for him.
No one called the MPs—the bar manager, a scarecrow named Zetak,
who was well provided for by grateful drunks, arranged cover and
transport to the hospital. The kid didn't lose his teeth or his stripes,
but certainly his nerve. He never returned. Simmons table remained
sacrosanct.

And this Sunday afternoon, Simmons was engaged in more than just
drinking. He was stewing with remorse, and cursing his own stupidity.
He had screwed-up big time, telling that shave-tail Louey to shut up
and shoving him out of the way when he was pulling Wing CQ duty last
month. Not that the punk didn't deserve it.

They called it insubordination. Now Simmons was looking at retirement at twenty years or a court-martial. His choice. At least they gave
him that. Given the history in his Unfavorable Information Folder, he
was lucky they didn't bust him again and boot him out without waiting. He knew it, and they knew it. Simmons hadn't planned to retire
at twenty—only two months away—he'd planned to have a hell of a
celebration and stay in until he reached twenty-four.

From that vantage point, and that state of mind, he watched the drama unfold at the bar.

Rosie had blown in like a blue norther, sudden and unexpected, pausing a moment at the door and squinting into the dim room before she made her way to the bar. Although she was no more than five foot tall, and twenty pounds to the quarter, no one would mistake her for a child. Built like a brick outhouse, when she shook her mane of red hair, flashed her green eyes, and smoothed her pink polka-dotted dress down along her hips, she had the full attention of every man in the room.

"Hot damn, check that out ... hey, honey, come sit here ... hey, sweetheart, is it true, all that stuff about redheads" ... and on. She was greeted with the unique enthusiasm of Sunday afternoon drunks—those for whom Sunday was an anathema, aside from being an uninterrupted daylong happy hour. She had smiled at those closest to the door as if pleased by their attention and then sashayed to the bar at the front of the room.

The crowd there parted like the Red Sea, every guy offering her his seat. She chose one smack dab in the middle, and leaning forward to seat herself on the red vinyl stool, gave Scotty, the barkeep, a stunning view. An exquisitely wrought gold cross dangling from a delicate chain guarded by deep, freckled cleavage that ended in shadowed mystery.

When seated, her tiny, strappy-sandaled feet didn't even touch the floor; and her charmeuse polyester dress, forget the deep V-neck that shouted out "Looky here, looky here," covered the rest of her body like snakeskin.

Huddled in the shadowy corner, Simmons nursed his scotch and studied Rosie's performance over the rim of his glass. He didn't have a lot of use for broads. Didn't have a lot of use for the world outside the motor pool, NCO club and his room in the non-com quarters. The old Master Sergeant claimed nowhere but the Air Force as home—and now he was losing that.

Raised by a single, buffet-Catholic mother, along with her *consort de jour*, he learned early on how things worked. His mom was a bartender at the Loggers' Lair, the only tavern in Drain, the small southern Oregon town where he grew up. They lived in a tiny furnished apartment above the bar, and he spent his formative years sitting at the top of the stairs, listening to randy jokes and boisterous laughter. Sometimes he wondered who his father was.

The redhead, with her drawl and Bible, held his attention. What the hell was a Bible thumper doing here? It pissed him off. Simmons' only religious education was Christmas and Easter masses during his childhood, seasoned by incense, sweet pinches on the cheek, and pats on the butt by the only father he ever was to know—and who was to know him.

He had no use for holier-than-thou, goody-goody broads. She sure as hell didn't belong here. How in hell did she even get on base? Who in hell let her in here? The hell with this. Simmons belched as he stood, raised his glass, sucked up the dregs and headed for the bar. He was going to set her straight. He was almost beside her when she began to cough.

Her unblemished porcelain face paled even more. "Excuse me." Still coughing, Rosie covered her mouth with her left hand, displaying a miniscule diamond ring and a livid scar on the back of her hand that ran up and around her wrist as if delineating the path of an errant flame. It appeared to snake its way under her long shiny sleeves. "I really do need a drink." Her short fingernails, filed smooth and covered with clear polish, seemed incongruent with her now-smudged deep burgundy lipstick. "It's my allergies—they always kick up when I gets around cigarette smoke." She coughed again, then grabbed a bar napkin and wiped her nose.

Simmons, ignoring her distress, shouldered his way through the hopefuls now surrounding her, elbowed the guy on the stool next to her and motioned him off. Then he eased his way onto it and waggled his eyebrows at Scotty. "Yeh, Scotsman, ya got any *ahra cee Colah* for this little lady? She looks like she needs it *real* bad. Might stop her coughing and shut her the hell up." He pushed a strand of oily hair off his forehead.

Rosie glared, teary eyed, into his weathered face. "Honey, you pokin' fun at me?" She swiped at one eye with the back of her hand and used the bar napkin to blow her nose.

Simmons smirked and licked his lips. His voice got louder. "Now that's an idea ... No. But it could be arranged." He paused, waiting for his audience to join in.

Instead, the group at the bar sidled off. Some snickered. Nervous. A few of the drunks sitting at tables grinned. Others barely chuckled. Two old guys at the end of the bar snorted then fell silent.

The redhead stiffened and looked him straight in the eyes. "That's not nice. Rosie's goin' to have to teach you a lesson." She pulled her purse off her shoulder, opened it, and tucked her makeup and Bible back inside. Then she swung around and faced Simmons head-on.

"Sweeten this up a bit, Scotsman." Simmons pushed his glass toward the barkeep while he watched, his face split in a wide snarky smile; Simmons rarely took any woman seriously. Not since his first experience.

At fourteen, Simmons was the biggest kid in ninth grade, the only one with significant body hair and a budding moustache. His height and weight were commensurate and developmentally precocious—all in all, he was a total package—most of the girls wanted to check it out. While they thought he was playing hard to get, in truth, he was shy and didn't know what to think about the female sex—until he fell in love.

The small Drain high school hired a new P.E. teacher that same year. Not much to look at, Amanda Knowles had been a dweeb in high school, working hard to maintain scholarship grades, and college was no different. Amanda worked hard for her "B" average, and toiled at a part-time job in the dean's office to pay her tuition. She'd never had a love life—not even a boyfriend. She arrived without creds, except being able to teach P.E., and remedial math. That made her a prize in that part of the state.

It wasn't much of a stretch for her to notice Simmons. She admired his body in the gym, and nurtured his brain in math ... nurturing his sexual development was just another aspect of teaching.

Simmons had a sweet deal until he got caught with a cigarette in the boys' bathroom. It went south when a teacher walked in; he tossed the butt into the trashcan and set it on fire. He looked to Amanda for help—she didn't know him. So much for counting on a woman.

After his suspension, lectures from the principal and school counselor and rants from his mother, he decided to forgo tobacco; he moved on to pot. This time, when he got caught, he was expelled—small town equaled small minds equaled no tolerance for aberrant behavior.

He enlisted in the Army when he turned eighteen. Given the choice of a year in jail or join up, both he and the judge agreed the army was the better option. "Make a man out of you," opined the judge. "Teach you to leave other people's property alone, and keep your hands to yourself."

"You got a Colt 45 in that purse somewhere? What's wrong, twerp—can't find your gun? Well, *honey*, I'll let you grab mine. I got it right here."

Given all his previous crudeness toward women who had ventured into the bar, this remark was in keeping with Simmons' behavior. But today it seemed out of line. The young redhead deserved better—the other guys in the bar, some red-faced, others shaking their heads, turned away from the couple, staring into their drinks or out into the smoke-dim barroom as if contemplating the meaning of life.

In the Army, Simmons learned the real facts of life. Women liked to trade. They never gave anything for free, but sex for cigarettes was almost free, and sharing heroin or speed was good for a couple days of revelry. He learned other things too; In Vietnam, he was the go-to guy if he had enough product. His gold project was most profitable. As a Graves Registration Specialist, he learned how to mine gold from casualties—gold teeth, wedding rings, religious medals—didn't matter the item, as long as it was gold. He snagged every bit he could off any dead comrade, and stashed it in an empty coffin until he had enough for a good sale. Simmons was a survivor. He returned to the United States loaded with cash, crabs and cynicism, and re-upped in the Air Force since he already knew how to fly.

"Where you from? You talk funny." Rosie turned and hard-eyed the bartender. "Don't he? Don't he talk funny?"

Simmons watched her in the mirror behind the bar and smiled. Then he rubbed his hand over his Sunday afternoon stubble. He never shaved on weekends except when he had duty. Weekends were for drinking, gambling and sometimes getting lucky with one of the skanks who hung around the NCO club like blowflies on a carcass. Down here in San Antonio, that kind of woman found his manner of speech appealing, not *funny*—the fact that he had no accent made him seem more cultured than the rednecks they knew. He wondered if she'd ever had a whisker burn. He'd like to give her one—to top off the weekend— share a little of his misery.

"Where you from?" Rosie persisted. "You really do talk funny. What you talkin', Mister? Your gun? You talkin' dirty? Are you?" She thought about it, decided. "Mister, you should be ashamed—no—you should be scared," she said. "Evildoers are trapped by their sinful talk, and so the innocent escape trouble. Proverbs 12:13." Rosie reached out and touched his hand. "You ever been saved?"

He needed to set this broad straight. With both hands, stubby fingers splayed, Simmons pushed away from the bar, scooting his stool back enough to accommodate his barrel chest. When he swiveled around, his face, etched by the sun, with a thin scar on the left side that zigzagged from his hairline down into his eyebrow, was red with rage. He was about to let her have it. No broad talked to him like that. Ashamed? Hell no. She should be ashamed, waltzing in here, playing innocent, holier than thou. Damned phony bitch. Scared? In a rat's ass. He opened his mouth—then shut it when his gut twisted and roared. "You wait right here I want to talk to you about *scared*." Simmons slid off the stool and stood, flexing his thick arms and rolling his shoulders, before he shuffled toward the head.

"Excuse me ... miss?" Scotty sounded conciliatory, "No offense, but why are you here? I mean, are you old enough to be in a bar? And, what with your allergies and all, is this a good place for you to be?" He paused, as if struck by a different thought. "For that matter, how did you even get on base?

"Oh, that was easy." She laughed and it was as if someone opened a window and let in the sunshine. "My cousin Jo Bob invited us. Ever since I been saved, I been waiting for the chance to go to a bar. Today was it." Rosie was bobbing her right foot and wiggling on the stool. "My daddy and me come to dinner with Joe Bob. He's a cook here—just finished his training. This was his first Sunday dinner, so he done invited us. He arranged for us to come on base." Rosie beamed at the barkeep. "Weren't that nice? He shore did a bang-up job … course, I reckon he just kinda hepped out, bein's he's a brand new cook … but it was a mighty fine meal." Her voice lowered to intimate and conspiratorial. "I just waited till e'body was full and praisin' Joe Bob, and then slipped away. They didn't even notice. I seen this place on the way to the mess hall. How come they call it that, anyhow? Weren't no messes I could see—looked right tidy to me." She frowned, just enough for cute.

Rosie grabbed another napkin and began shredding it. "Ever since I been saved, I been waiting for the chance to go to a bar." She smiled, displaying startlingly white teeth, tiny, like a toddler's. "My pastor says I got the callin'. I been blessed with the Word, and it's my duty to be here, to convert sinners, make them give up their evil ways. You been saved? Been baptized?" Her green eyes lasered him, almost forcing him backward with their intensity.

In the bathroom, Simmons lingered at the sink. He rinsed his face with cold water and then examined it in the mirror. His full head of hair—good genes from his Scandinavian mother—tarnished brass shot with streaks of gray, was as long as the regs allowed. His leathery cheekbones and jaw were pale under a patina of dissipation, exposure and cigarette smoke. He needed to sit down. Pretty soon, there'd be no more Sundays at the club, no one to move aside when he stepped up to the bar. He looked around the head, as if to commit it to memory. After all these years, they were pushing him out. And for what? Letting that little ass know who was really in charge. He thought that was why they assigned him to assist the Officer of the Day—why in hell else did they need a Wing NCOIC? Wasn't his fault. His gut twisted. Once again, Simmons knelt before the toilet and vomited.

He flushed the toilet and sat on the seat, fighting waves of nausea and the urge to scream. Fear, bubbling up from some long unused part of his brain surged into the frontal lobes, mixing with anger, creating rage. He wanted to hurt someone. He wanted to cry. He wanted …

The scotch, though purged from his stomach, still raged through his body, fueling his angst.

He thought about the broad. Coming' in here where she doesn't belong, flashing her Bible along with her tits, going on about saving people. *You ever been saved?* Really! Who does she think she is? Saving people. Like she could save anybody … save him. Stupid. Stupid idea. What the hell does that mean, anyway? Saved? "Ain't nobody can save my ass now," he proclaimed to the face in the mirror.

Simmons grabbed a paper towel and wiped his nose.

Wonder if people really get saved? That little ol' gal sure seemed to think so. She smelled pretty good, though. Sweet. Like roses, maybe. "Wonder what it's like to be saved," Simmons mused. "Wonder if that could help me now." His stomach gave another lurch, sending him back to the toilet. His head was spinning when he struggled to his feet again. "If I keep this up, I won't make it to retirement." Simmons rinsed his mouth at the sink, then checked his teeth in the mirror, grimaced back at the bloodshot eyes. Wonder, if I got saved … if a sweet little thing like that would ever go for a guy like me. He almost said it out loud, then did say, "I'd like to get to know …" He looked at himself again and frowned. "Don't kid yourself, loser. Once you're out on the street, you're nobody, and ain't nobody gonna give a shit—and ain't nuthin' can save you.

He felt another surge of anger. "No. What I'd really like to do is get in her pants, but she'd probably turn me in … have me strung up by my … oh, hell. Who needs it? Broads like her are nuthin' but trouble." He stroked his chin again. Probably shoulda shaved this morning. He wiped his eyes and mouth once more.

When he returned to the bar, he was ready for battle.

"Well, took you long enough. I been waitin' for you. Now we gonna get started." Not waiting for his response, the redhead rotated on the stool and faced the motley group habituating the bar. "Y'all need to snuff out them smokes and put down them drinks now. Rosie here is goin' to give y'all a little talkin' to." She picked up the Bible and held it above her head. "I want y'all to looky here at this book. You see this book? Any y'all ever read it? Ever been saved?"

"What the hell do you think you're doin'?" Simmons bellowed. He stepped toward her—then stopped when she focused on him.

She stared him down. "You don't look so good, Mister. You feelin' bad? You needin' to get right with the Lord? He's right there beside you, waitin'. You feel Him? You see Him?" Her tiny voice shrilled. "Y'all, eva'body, you feel Him? He's right here, waitin' for you. Just ask him in … say hallelujah. Go on, say it!" Rosie raised the Bible with her right hand, as if it were a fist. "Hallelujah! Praise God."

"Lady." Scotty came out from behind the bar and touched her shoulder. "Lady. You can't be doing that in here. This is a club. You have to leave." He tried to take her arm.

Rosie shook him off. "Didn't you hear me? I done told you, I gots the call." Rosie set the Bible on the bar and held out her arm. "You see this here scar?" She pushed her sleeve up so it was more visible. "It's a sign. God saved me from a fire. I was just a baby, but he marked me so's I'd know ... He done saved me for a reason." She looked upward and smiled. "I heard Him talkin'. He done said, 'Go forth and save sinners.' So's I a'gonna save me some sinners here today." She began to cough again. "This here is where I been sent ... here ... this den of iniquity ... to save ya'll." She picked up the Bible and turned back to the men in the bar. "Y'all hear me? You're mine. I been sent for you. And I ain't leavin' 'till y'all come around—till y'all confess your sins and get right with the Lord." She shook the Bible at them. "It's all in here. What y'all gots to do."

Her coughing increased, reddening her face and bringing tears to her eyes. They began trickling down her cheeks, creating pinky-orange rivulets, dripping into her cleavage. Making a mewling sound, she fell to her knees, clasping the Bible in both hands, as if imploring the onlookers to action. "Please, ya'll—do it for me, I needs to ..." The coughing choked off the rest of her words. She fell forward, seemingly unconscious.

Scotty was dialing 911 when the old man came into the bar. He looked like a dry-dirt farmer, wearing striped overalls and a blue work shirt Sunday morning clean, and brogans Shinola bright and carrying a limp straw hat held in one hand. "Ah. There she be." He looked where Rosie lay, pale, breathing so shallow as to be almost indiscernible, and then around at the now mostly sober drunks. "My daughter—ya'll have to forgive her—she's bad sick. Has these here spells ... sometimes seems she gonna die." He dropped his hat, stepped on it in his hurry to reach Rosie. "My God. She dead? My Rosie dead?"

The drinkers muttered to one another, some averted their eyes. Dead? Hell if they knew. Not their business. Besides, Scotty had called the medics—he always did when things came up. Some returned to their drinks. Others stood around and watched. The old man was doing just fine.

Simmons lit up and inhaled. He watched Rosie's father cradle her shoulders and rock back and forth, mumbling encouragement and crooning in her ear, while they waited for the paramedics.

The old man began to babble. "Convertin' sinners. 'S what'll cure her. 'S what she thinks. Brother Jones—you know—the one on Channel Two, Sunday mornin's? He done told her. She sent him a letter, beggin' to be healed. This here—convertin' folks like ya'll—'s what he told her she had to do ... and ... and now?"

Maybe she wasn't a phony. What if she really was sick? She was a puny little thing. He took another drag off his cigarette. What if it was true, she could help me. What if she could, but instead she died? Tears blurred his vision as he exhaled, and began to leak onto his cheeks. His heart fluttered as if trying to escape a trap, and the floor shifted under his feet. What the hell? Simmons closed his eyes and inhaled deeply.

"Fellers?" The old man's voice cracked as he addressed the men in the bar. "Pray for her? Till help comes ... please, just pray?"

None of the bystanders moved. They just looked at him as if he had taken leave of his senses.

"Aw, hell." Simmons snuffed his cigarette out. "C'mon you guys, let's do it. Can't hurt none. Maybe it will even help. Least, that's what he thinks. Who wants to start?" He stepped over and with thumb and fore-finger, picked up the Bible from the floor beside Rosie. He held it away from his body as if it were a rattler, and tried to hold it steady. "Okay, e'body ... Hallelujah?" It sounded like a question.

"Anyone got a camera? ... Sheesh, Simmons' gone soft. ... Sit down and shut up, Simmons ... Simmons, you turned pussy?" the voices surrounded him, interspersed with laughter, mocking.

"Knock it off, you bozos." Simmons glared at the two old guys at the bar until they put down their glasses and nodded. Then turned his ire toward the rest of the drinkers—none would meet his eyes. He checked the twit. She was very pale. Had stopped coughing. Was she even breathing? His stomach clenched.

"C'mon, now." He looked around the room. No one was laughing—they were all watching him, some smirking, some silent and cautious—and some just curious.

"All together, now. Praise the Lord. Hallelujah! Sir, if you're listenin', ya gotta heal that little girl. Okay? Hallelujah, Praise the Lord." This time his voice was a bit louder, like he had an inside straight and was saying, "I'll call and raise ..."

His stunned cohorts watched in amazement. They knew him. Simmons was an old war dog of the first degree. Always close to being busted, always walking on the edge. Like a fourteen year old, impulse-controlled, hormone driven boy living in an aging, battered warrior's body, he just couldn't stay away from booze and dope, or out of trouble. His only god was the god of war and his only bible was a tattered copy of Kinsey's book about women that he picked up at a poker game in boot camp, read before he went to Viet Nam, and had used as a reference ever since.

"C'mon, you dirty lechers. Say it! Say it now—hallelujah, praise the Lord." Now he sounded like he was pleading.

Simmons pleading?

Feet shuffled, butts shifted on chairs, and silence prevailed. They were embarrassed for Simmons, him with the worn stripes of his present status dwarfing outlines of stripes earned and lost over the years, like an acne scar that would never fade—the metaphor for his life.

"Oh, what the hell." Another old Master Sergeant, known for his ability to swill beer, gave it up. He too had felt something—an epiphany of sorts. Simmons was pitiful. "C'mon, guys. Can't hurt nothing." He croaked out a passable "praise the lord."

"Louder," Simmons ordered.

Scotty watched wide-eyed as one after another, the grogs fell into line, with more than a modicum of nervous laughter, and began to shout. "Hallelujah, Praise the Lord!" The place was beginning to rock when he called the MPs.

The crisis forgotten, the medics forgotten, the room was reverberating with praise and prayers. The men were grinning, trying to outdo one another, getting into the action. Some were even pounding on tables, creating a cadence for the mantra, so caught up, and having so much fun. They were just short of a brawl when the MPs arrived.

In the ensuing confusion, they forgot about the woman ... forgot about Simmons, focused on pandemonium. It was the most exciting Sunday afternoon in memory. One for the books.

Even for Simmons.

When Rosie stirred slightly in her father's arms, slowly opened her eyes and surreptitiously looked around the room, he caught his breath. She was alive. There was hope. His heart raced. There was HOPE. Remnants of Glen Fiddich oozing out his pores, his head murky with pain, and eyes filled with anticipation, Simmons fell to his knees before her. "Is it true? I can be saved? I'll do anything ..."

While Simmons was wiping his tears away, Rosie looked at her father and winked.

Wall

Mercedes Lawry

I tried scrambling over the wall
but it's too slick, too fraught
with alibis and clever narratives
that spill their guts so you find yourself
weeping and unable to get a toehold.

Damn, I said, damn this wall
that makes us all nervous and willing
to placate their holier-than-thou majesties
just so we can get a cold potato
and keep the photo of our dead dog
under our worn down pillows
as if that was a high sign for compassion.

I tried more than once to climb over
that wall, in the early morning fog,
when the babies are starting to murmur,
in the hollow night when every dream
has packed up and jumped ship,
in a blinding rain, thinking I might swim over
on a miracle flood, in an early June wind
that could preoccupy anyone with its sweet pretense.

We have forgotten what's on the other side of the wall,
but we haven't forgotten what the sun looks like
when it falls into the black sea or what happens to seeds
when you plant them in the earth
and give them light and water.

Ribbons

Tricia Cantillon

The only photo I have of me and Bertha is one from Christmas morn-ing, probably 1972 or 1973. I am on the living room floor opening a "Play-N-Jane" doll and she is sitting in a chair behind me, bows from opened presents adorn her white uniform dress. She has several strands of leftover ribbon in her hand. My dad sits to her right and my sister to her left. She's in the middle of everything, just where she likes it.

1. When Bertha and I wait at the bright pink bus stop outside the Beverly Hills Hotel, she reminds me to "act young." Children under five ride for free in 1971. Being six, the only thing I can think of is to suck my thumb. The 91-S rolls slowly to the curb and the doors swing open. Bertha grabs my hand and pulls me up the tall, black rubber steps behind her. She's counted out her bus fare already and it plinks its way down the metal hole into the belly of the change holder. "Morning, Sir," she always says to the driver. She looks down at me, doing my best impersonation of a five year old, "Come on, Baby."

We move sideways down the aisle so as not to bump into other pas-sengers. Bertha picks our seats and, using her hip, slides me over next to the window. She promises I can pull the string to ring the buzzer that lets the driver know we want off at the next stop. She'll have to help me climb onto my seat so I can reach the cord hanging above the window. And she'll make sure I remember to only pull once.

2. The basement in the Broadway is like most department stores, it's home to Kitchenwares, Appliances, and Toys. Bertha and I hold hands as we ride the escalator down two floors from the handbags section. We're both wearing black shoes. Mine are patent leather Mary Jane's. Bertha's are low-heeled shoes that have laces.

Although I'd like to take a sharp right turn and make a beeline to the dolls and board games, I know we're going straight to Appliances, where a long row of color and black and white TVs are lined up next to each other. Many look like the models I have seen on game shows. They are like long tables with screens and large dials. Bertha paces a bit before positioning us in front of the largest set on display. She changes the channel and then checks her watch. We've made it, just in time. The screen goes dark after a commercial and then we see them. Dr. Steve is in his office with Nurse Jessie. They talk about something and then the words "General Hospital" appear. This is Bertha's program and we will stand here for the entire thirty minutes and watch. She will brush off attempts by the salesman to interest her in purchasing a TV, while making sure the volume is at a level where she can hear it. If we have to stand too close we'll hurt our eyes. This is not our first visit to an Appliance section to watch her show, and it won't be our last. The world stops at 2:00 pm, no matter where she is or what she is doing.

One time, when my dad forgot his house key, she yelled at him. "Why are you banging on my bell when my program is on?" I liked that he knew what it was like to get in trouble.

3. Glendale Savings and Loan is just down the street from Swensen's, the only place I know that has ice cream with gumballs in it. The bank is at the corner of Beverly Drive and Wilshire. If you look straight up when you stand in front of it, there's colored glass that lines the top. It looks like hard candies in a dark bowl.

We don't usually go to the bank, but I guess Bertha needs to cash a check, which I am familiar with, because one of the things I do most often with Mom is go to the bank to cash checks. We wait our turn to sit opposite a man at a desk. He and Bertha are talking and I am not listening until she hands me a little blue plastic case that says "Glendale Savings & Loan" on the front. "Do you know what this is?" I shake my head. It sort of reminds me of the tiny prayer books we got in our First Communion purses last year. She opens it and I see that it says "$1,100." "This is your savings account, Baby. I started it, you add to it as you get older. But you cannot spend it. You need to save." I felt very grown up in that moment with my important looking bank book-thingy and knowing I had a thousand dollars. Even though I am eight, I know that Bertha's gift is a big deal. "Bertha loves money," my mom tells me, when I recount going to her apartment and seeing all the birthday cards she'd received, all filled with cash.

4. It's been about three years since we've seen Bertha. My parents officially separated and we sold our house in 1977. Now we need to call and tell her my dad died. Even though he was only fifty-three, his death is not a shock to us. He's battled to get sober for years. I tell myself he had a long life and he's much better off now. But I'm sad he'll never see me drive a car or know if Jimmy Carter will be re-elected. Bertha is sorry to hear the news. Although they butted heads often, she had a deep affection for him and he for her. Her Christmas gift to our family one year was three pastel portraits: one of me, one of my dad, and one

of Jesus.

I'm standing at the back of the line, behind my mom, my two brothers and two sisters, the casket and Monsignor Sullivan. I've been in this church a thousand times and everyone here is friends or family but I feel like I'm looking through the bottom of an empty glass until I see her. Bertha is in the front pew, which has been reserved for family, right where she knows she belongs.

We are filing into limousines that will caravan to the cemetery. I am waiting for the man from the mortuary to tell me where to go. He directs me to the first car. As I'm climbing in, I look to see who is going in the second car and there is Bertha sitting in the front seat of the limousine next to the driver. She's in her white crocheted hat with the dangling tassels, a huge smile on her face. Bertha loves a good funeral.

5. For the next twelve or so years Bertha joins us for Thanksgiving and Christmas. One of my sister's childhood friends is now an actor on General Hospital. He joins us for several holidays as well. Bertha never calls him by his real name, Kin, but calls him "Scotty," the character he portrays, "Scotty, you want more peas?" In her apartment near the Robert Kennedy and Martin Luther King posters is a photo collage from her 85th birthday, a smiling Bertha, cheek to cheek with "Scotty."

6. "Hi Baby, how you feel?" This is how she greets me when I come into her room at the nursing home. She's had a small stroke and the doctors won't let her go home. She is one of those people who will wither without her independence, but she is unsafe living alone. I fold the crocheted blanket that's on the edge of her bed. She's uncharacteristically quiet, sitting in her wheelchair. Someone has French braided her hair, which has completely transformed her looks, and she's wearing brand new Nike athletic shoes. "Where did you get those fancy things?" She looks at her feet and shrugs.

I chatter about the plans I'm making for my wedding in September, I'm not sure if Bertha's listening, but I can't bear the silence. Even though I'm a grown twenty-eight year old woman and she has just turned 96, I am longing for her to boss me about, tell me to find her wallet, or a pen, a tissue, in the bottomless pit that is her pocketbook. Finally, a nurse comes to get her for physical therapy and I push her down to the rehab room.

Bertha's reluctant at first, but they get her up on the apparatus that looks like super low parallel bars. She holds the rails and follows the therapist's instruction. "Wow, that's great!" She's raising one leg at a time. The stiff, new shoes look absurd on her feet, but she's smiling from ear to ear. I find comfort and relief in her smile. I am not ready for her to be frail, or needy.

It's about a month before my wedding. Quinton stands when he sees me come in the back door. He tells me to sit down. My mom called. Bertha died. Not unexpected but definitely un-welcome news. I smile, remembering how she always said she "longed for her eternal home."

She planned her memorial down to the last detail. She's laid in an open pink casket at the front of the church. Her "brothers" and "sisters" give testimony to her generosity, unshakeable faith and devotion to God. She'd given a young man money for community college. She baked 7-Up cakes for neighbors. She prayed for the sick. This glimpse into the life she led away from our family makes me all the more lonesome for her. "You're the Baby!" I hear more than once. And I realize she *never* called me by name.

7. I'm in the kitchen preparing coffee for the morning when I spy a cupboard door that's slightly ajar, a drawer that's still open. I move to close them and stop.

"Mason! Georgia! Can you come here?" Like me, at their age, they are melodramatic and fussy as they drag their six and eight year old bodies back into the kitchen. Their shoulders slouch, their arms swing at their sides. "What?" They sigh in unison. Georgia looks at her brother, certain he is to blame for whatever is coming. "Close that drawer and the cabinet, please." They groan as quietly as they can before obliging, then shuffle out—puzzled by what has just happened. They are clearly wondering why I couldn't have just done it myself. I was standing right there. In the months and years to come they'll be summoned from the backyard, from video games, even from sleep. And it will be Bertha's voice that calls them.

Crows Strutting

Emily Strauss

crows— sleek of head, fine
black feathers lying flat
strut through gutters
parks, dry fountains, waste

bins, they prance, cock
their heads, eye the tasty
bits, prance, man, *prance*
with them stick legs

and deep breast, glossy
coats in the broken glass
torn take-out boxes
thick bills delicately

probing like at the pawn
shop where we comb
the tray of necklaces
nothing suits

and that caw, man, fat
black horn *caw*, cool
player on his sax, jazz
guy trumpeting

another pile of trash, dirty
wrappers, black brothers
march on, strut their cool
stuff, nodding sagely

The Ecliptic Principle

Pamela Hanson

I'm not sure why I didn't wrestle Dorothy to the ground when I saw her leaving with the bronze armillary I'd set aside for purchase at the church bazaar. I was in the middle of telling Harriet's niece about my knee replacement when I spied her bustling out the door, looking as though she'd found a piece of Noah's Ark itself.

I've asked her on several occasions to allow me to buy it, at a sizable markup I might add, but she refused to even consider my offers. I must have been crazy to think she would treat me with kind regard since this is hardly the first thing she's stolen from me.

Her thievery began early in life at Creekside Grammar School when she absconded with my best friend, Lula, who had moved here from Charlotte. I told Miss Granger I'd be happy to show Lula around the school, paying particular attention to the location of the girls' bathrooms and nurse's office. No more than two hours had elapsed since her arrival when Dorothy wheedled her way into Lula's good graces, offering to escort her through the lunch line.

Dorothy lived with the delusion that she had a special rapport with the lunch ladies and could procure extra servings with a mere smile. In truth, fewer portions of those bland-tasting mashed potatoes, smothered with a brown gelatinous substance, would have done her ample figure a world of good.

But as we all know, bonding over food is a powerful experience and Lula was permanently attached to Dorothy's side after one trip through the line. Now that I think about it, Lula could have stood to drop a few pounds herself.

Later, on the playground, Lula tried to make up for deserting me. I politely declined to join her and Dorothy in a game of hopscotch. I have never taken kindly to being a third wheel.

Our relationship, or lack thereof, continued in high school. Dorothy, or "Dot" as she then liked to be called, practiced cartwheels on the grass in the community park, her blouse riding up so as to threaten exposing her bosom. It never quite made it to that point, however, lest every boy watching see it was stuffed with enough tissue to single-handedly meet the needs of every head cold sufferer this side of the Mississippi.

"She can't help that she's pretty," Mother said one evening when I mentioned the display Dot had put on for an upperclassman seated expectantly on the park bench. My father had glanced up from his paper at the mention of her name.

I continued despite Mother's protest. "I would think she'd be afraid all the tissue she uses to stuff her you-know-what would fall out."

"Oh, I don't think Dorothy stu—"

We never heard the rest of what my father had to say on this point as my mother cut short his comment with a glare that could have stopped the Huns from invading.

Naturally, Dot's peppy acrobatics won her the spot of head cheerleader. Never mind that my round-offs were legendary. They were no match for cartwheels and mounds of well-placed tissue.

I was assigned a spot at one end of the cheer lineup. Mother assured me it wasn't Dot's fault and was merely a result of us being arranged by height. That was a lie. I noticed Mother always sided against me in matters concerning Dorothy. People still do. It's as though they're bewitched by her. Thankfully, I'm immune.

Dottie, as she decided to be called in college, continued to seize whatever interested her. While I was busy pursuing a degree in Home Economics, she was busy becoming a popular coed. Sororities and fraternities alike adored her, which was understandable. She didn't just take, but gave. Money, and if necessary, herself.

She certainly had John Phillips spellbound. He and I had become something of an item during sophomore year. Little did I realize that giving in to John's persistent requests to meet Dottie would result in his deciding we were no longer "right for each other." His gullibility was disgraceful, her bewitching, unseemly.

After stealing and dating John for nearly a year, she didn't even have the decency to marry him when he asked. And why would she? Dottie had readjusted her sights. They were now on William Davis, a senior whose father managed the largest bank in the state. "Why swill beer when you can sip champagne?" I overheard her saying at a campus mixer.

Upon graduation, I began praying the newly married Mr. and Mrs. Davis would establish residency in the capital to aid in his run for governor. Due to the untimely death of his father, William was promoted to bank president, and so the newlyweds remained in town.

Dorothy, back to using her formal name since she felt it more befitting the wife of a wealthy bank official, insisted she and William buy the monstrosity of a house next to Harold's and my English Tudor. It was no surprise that Mother and Father were overjoyed when I delivered the news.

This proximity of our dwellings meant our children would attend the same schools, giving her further opportunity to make my life miserable. Admittedly, those were some of our darker years.

Consider the time Dorothy graciously withdrew from the race for President and settled on a lesser position of Secretary-Treasurer of the Gramercy Parent-Teacher Association. She claimed it was because she had learned so much from her husband about record keeping, but she and I both knew it was because she'd been tipped off about the school principal's dissatisfaction over the PTA's decision to spend money on band equipment rather than the football field. She was hoping I'd get swallowed up in the impending controversy. As it was, I managed through the turmoil during my two-year term, but not without a loss of many nights' sleep and several friends.

Or consider the time she and her husband tried to blackball Harold and me from joining the local country club. She assured me it was a misunderstanding in the membership balloting process, but I wasn't fooled. I had her number from a very early age.

Or the time she violated the County Fair rules by using her own hybrid berries instead of the specified blue, boysen, or raspberries. She was awarded First Place for her "Dotberry" pie in spite of her blatant disregard for propriety.

The write up on the front page of The Gazette was courtesy of the editor, who was also presiding officer of the aforementioned country club, which Dorothy and her husband sponsored by writing a generous check each year. The featured article included not only a picture of her holding a piece of the pie with "Just the right balance of sweetness and tartness," but also the award-winning recipe. I refused to eat a piece when Mother made it.

The one thing I was thankful for through these tumultuous years was my Harold. He never doubted the wrath Dorothy inflicted on me. He was as steadfast as my father's old hunting dog.

Harold would walk next door on the occasions when I'd taken just about all I could from Dorothy. He'd return a half-hour or so later, relating to me how he'd told her that she'd treated me unfairly and that he had half a mind to speak with William when he got home from his banking duties.

I've given it thorough consideration and have decided that recovering my stolen armillary from Dorothy will serve to right so many of the wrongs she has inflicted on me. I take delight in knowing she will soon feel what it is like to have something taken from her, without warning, without hope of restitution.

I wish I could be there to see the look on her face when she notices the bare spot on her front lawn. Naturally, I will have to display my rightful acquisition somewhere out of public view, but it's a small price to pay for the joy it will bring me.

I remember the scene as if it were yesterday. The first time I saw it. I was late and he was standing in the center of an astronomy classroom at the university, lecturing. He turned at the sound of my footsteps. A smile emerged as he removed his hand from the armillary he was using to explain the principle of the ecliptic. At the end of class, he walked over and introduced himself. It was at that moment Professor Harold George Fredrickson stole my heart.

Experiments in Male Vanity

Daniel Pecchenino

These experiments in male vanity
have yielded decidedly mixed results.

The summer of white legs and lies
sailed down the gutter in boat shoes.

The winter of mechanical prowess
caused chemical burns inside and out.

The spring of sensitive seduction
suffered from a lack of sensitivity.

But the fall of avian preening
saw something unexpected, a little

bird chirping back, impressed enough
by this jangly display to sit still

on the wire awhile and laugh
along with the sappy sucker

puffing his way through notes
unknown until they were sung.

Missing in Action

Dorothy Place

He lay on his back, uniform muddied, helmet lost, rifle at ready, as if pointing toward an unseen enemy. Missing in action, Harold thought as he scooped the toy soldier up out of the dirt, and wiped him clean with his red kerchief. Poor lost guy reminded him of his brother, James and his army men. That was what he had called his toy soldiers, army men. That was a long time ago. A doleful smile saddled Harold's thin lips as he eased James from his mind, placed the toy on the garage windowsill, and continued trenching for the new sewer line he was installing. The day darkened and shadows lengthened, the shovel grated against the clay soil, carelessly casting its steady cadence into the air. The soldier stood at ready, surveying the scene for incoming ordinance, waiting for orders to leave his post.

Harold was a few days short of finishing the trenching job. His wife, Martha had wanted him to hire a day worker from down at the gas station, but he refused, insisted that he could do the job. She had gotten that look, the one she wore when disgruntled. The soft, round cheeks he once touched with affection cemented into lines of reproach. "You'll kill yourself," she said. "It's too hot out there, and you're not as young as you used to be." Her words, as harsh as the clay ground, pierced the lampshade, the drapes, his brown recliner chair, and his heart.

Now that he was retired, she reminded him of his age and told him that he couldn't do this or couldn't do that. Christ, you'd think he was on his deathbed. That was the way it was between them. Fingernails grating against the blackboard. Just another battleground. Neither side willing to give in. She was right, though. Digging a trench was one hell of a job. Some help would be nice, but he wouldn't say so. Not to her, anyway.

After breakfast each day, he'd go out to the back yard, rub the sore spot on his lower back, and ease himself into the trench. The number on the windowsill grew to almost platoon size. Several foot soldiers as well as two scouts with palm fronds in their helmets, one machine-gun carrier, and a radio man, his battery pack complete except for the antenna that had been lost in some past skirmish. He even found an army nurse, still clutching her black medical bag in one hand. Her once white uniform was permanently stained, but the insignia on her cap flashed like a beacon. Bright red. A spot of cheer in the cold, damp earth.

Whenever Harold's energy sagged and he thought he'd quit for the day, he'd look over at his growing army. The possibility of adding to his collection cheered him. Just a few more shovelfuls, he'd say to himself. Planes flew overhead, cars passed the house, the neighbor returned from work, slamming closed the garage door, but Harold didn't notice. The trenching job had become a rescue operation. He worked more slowly, searched for bits of color in the brown earth. After all, he reasoned, these soldiers had been missing in action a long time. No need to add to their injuries with a cruel shovel cut. By the end of the week, three with flame- throwers, a tiny hand grenade, a stretcher, several helmets, a couple of howitzers, a truck and two jeeps had joined the group.

The more army men Harold found, the more images of James, six years younger, crowded into his thoughts. His brother's obsession with army men had begun during the final stages of his illness, when he, only eight years at the time, was first restricted to home, then to bed. The family had searched for things to keep him occupied those long, dreary January days, but it was Aunt Josie who got it right. She had bustled in one afternoon, her flowered wrap-around dress tightly cinched at her ample waist and her swollen ankles overflowing the edges of her sensible shoes. The dimples in her elbows deepened as she reached into the shopping bag fashioned out of old flour sacks, and pulled out a bag of plastic soldiers, about 150 of them. From then on, James had spent his last days carefully setting up battle lines and waiting for Harold to come home from school.

That was James' last winter. Harold recalled how, on his way home from school, his boots had broken queer-shaped holes in the thin covering of snow, revealing the browned summer grass curled into perpetual frowns, and how the setting sun turned the low-hanging birch limbs into crystal chandeliers. And when he reached the front door, how he stamped the snow off his feet, making enough noise to drown out his mother's voice saying the same thing every day. "Take your boots off before you come in. I just cleaned."

"War games?" James would yell when he heard Harold's footsteps, his voice tumbling down the hallway, brushing past the pictures of their grandparents and the antique vase resting on the tiny table with the grape vine legs, meeting Harold, who by then, was half way up the stairs.

Harold brought with him the fresh scent of soon-it-will-snow again into James' room. It briefly pushed against the fetid and stale air poisoning the wallpaper, bed coverings, and furniture, like a flash of cool brightness, like a promise. But only a flash, disappearing as quickly as promises not kept, as quickly as the smile on James' face when Harold

Dorothy Place   45

spoke.

"Got homework," he'd beg off. "Maybe tomorrow I won't have so much to do." Every day, however, there was another excuse. Girls or basketball. Something more important than playing with a bunch of army men.

A biting pain interrupted Harold's thoughts. He unclenched his fist. The plastic soldier he had been holding left a red indentation on his palm. He shook his hand, easing the small ache. No one ever told him what was wrong with James. If he had known how it would end, would he have kept his promises? But, how can you know such things? He'd feel better if he didn't have to relive those times, but the past is never past. The army men reminded him of James, his thin hands grasping the toy soldiers, eyes pleading for just one game.

Harold named his little army, "James's Marauders" after some World War II stories he'd read about the British fighting in Burma. James would like that. But then again, maybe not. He would be fifty-nine now, perhaps no longer interested in toy soldiers. But time didn't move for someone who dies. In Harold's memory, James stayed the same as last he saw him. Somehow the name, James' Marauders seemed right. Yes, Harold assured himself, James would like it.

When the windowsill could hold no more pieces, he squirreled them upstairs and hid them in the cedar chest in the guest bedroom, careful not to let his wife know what he was doing. He didn't want to explain their presence to Martha. She wouldn't understand. She wouldn't approve.

It wasn't always that way between them. She disapproving, he bewildered. In the beginning, she had made Harold feel good about almost everything. She picked him out at the homecoming game the fall of his third year at Syracuse. At least, that was his version of the how-we-met story. In any case, it was when the giddiness of the last, crisp days of autumn endowed students with the certainty that this would be the year they'd ace their exams, win all the football games, and fall in love. Martha wore a blue, double-breasted coat with a blue and gold scarf. Her adorable cheeks were a ruddy red that matched her lipstick and the stadium flags fluttering in the late morning breeze.

On a whim, he had purchased a large yellow "mum" and fastened it onto her coat. It was one of those things he did without thinking, without considering the consequences. Like he was saying, I love you and want to marry you even before I know your name. Thinking back, he wondered how it had happened. So unlike him. Perhaps it was the excitement. The warm autumn air. His willingness to forget that, in a few weeks, the icy wind would blow across the lake and freeze the campus into its dreary academic routine.

They married, children came and went, things changed between them. Although Harold couldn't quite remember exactly when. It may have been years ago, but became more noticeable recently, since he retired. Martha acting as though he were the enemy, invading her territory. When he got up from the sofa, she would scurry in, fluff the pillows, and "tut-tut" herself back to whatever his bad behavior had interrupted. If his empty glass remained on the coffee table, she'd wipe the ring, and with a self-pitying sigh, whisk the glass into the kitchen and into the dishwasher. And lunch. "Right in the middle of the day," she'd grouse, as if noon was an inappropriate time to eat. "I have to stop everything just to feed you." Of course he offered to do small things, like prepare the noon meal, but she'd bristle. "What, and have you leave a mess for me to clean up?" There was no pleasing her. The more effort he expended, the more she rebuffed him. Simply put, his presence added to her daily burden.

He had considered going back to work. It was only a little over a year since he left Wells Bros. Accounting Agency, so there might still be a place for him. Give him something to look forward to each day and his mind something solid to latch onto. A chance to hang out and talk guy-talk. He'd bring in a few extra bucks. Going back to work might be the best way to please his wife.

"Harry, good to hear from you," Stan, his former boss had said when Harold called. "Things aren't the same around here without you."

Encouraged, Harold had asked if Stan could arrange to have him come in a few days a week. He tried not to sound anxious, to suggest that he might be doing Stan a small favor by returning. "Of course," Harold assured him, "he wouldn't expect full pay. Just enough to keep my interest and help you out wherever I can."

The back-to-work idea had been a good one but, like so many plans made by mice and men, it didn't work out the way he wanted. It seemed that the new man hired to replace him had revamped the computer program Harold had developed. According to Stan, the new program was so efficient he was having trouble keeping the new guy busy. "But stop by," Stan invited Harold. "We'll have a drink and talk over old times."

"Good idea." Harold tried to sound upbeat. "I'll give you a call." He knew that call would never be made. Life in the office had gone on without him.

Harold had considered applying for a job as a greeter at Walmart, but waffled. He tried to visualize himself smiling and rolling a cart toward shoppers who probably pitied him, assuming financial need had forced him to take the job. Walmart would get him out of the house, but would do little for his pocketbook or his self-esteem. Then the trenching job came along, and now he had his little army.

Evenings, instead of watching television, he'd join his army in the guest bedroom. Needless to say, his wife didn't miss him. She had her programs and selecting which to watch each night was her prerogative. "After all," she defended her choices, "I work all day." True. She busied herself with her housework, the roses, a lot of shopping, and volunteer work. Half the time, Harold didn't know where she was.

As the years passed, he and Martha shared less and less. Oh, early on, when they discussed their plans, he had promised to go with her to visit her folks in Indiana, or on that long-awaited trip to Hawaii, but work was always an obstacle. "Wait until next year," he'd tell her. "Things will settle down on the job, I'll have fewer responsibilities." Then it was, "After the kids are out of college, there will be more money for things like that." And finally, "Wait until we retire. We'll have more time." He'd retired now but the relatives in Indiana are gone and, somewhere along the way, Martha lost interest in spending time in Hawaii. He couldn't remember when she stopped asking.

Up in the guest bedroom, he set up the army men in battle lines along the patterns in his grandmother's quilt. The foot soldiers and flamethrowers advanced between the red strips that defined the quilt's log cabin design. He camouflaged the flamethrowers with small branches from the redwood tree out front, and set out small stones as land mines. The lying-down men waited behind the bolster-bunkers for the enemy to come in range and the supply depot, near the foot of the bed, kept the jeeps and tanks out of range of the howitzers. The nurse, black medical bag in hand, waited in the hospital area for the casualties to arrive. From far up on the pillows, scouts overlooked the entire scene.

When the trenching job was completed, he looked around for something to keep him out of his wife's way. He wasn't ready for Walmart yet. It required a degree of sociability he wasn't prepared to extend to strangers. And the blue vests. Really, not for him. He thought of cleaning out the garage—that would make his wife happy, but the idea held little pleasure for him, not like working in the fresh air and smelling the moist earth. Perhaps raised beds for a vegetable garden. More digging would preserve his newly acquired muscle tone, and he could luck out and add to his soldier collection. A project like that would keep him away from his wife's disapproving looks.

He sketched out a garden in his mind. Peas and string beans staked along the back fence, tomatoes on the far side of the yard where they would get the most sun, leafy stuff close to the garage, protected from the afternoon heat. He'd use redwood for the raised beds, and get the tire on the wheelbarrow fixed so he could haul the soil delivered to the curb into the back yard. If things worked out, he'd plant a winter garden and, if his wife agreed, start a compost pile behind the garage. Once the garden was in, he'd use decomposed granite to make walkways between the beds. Maybe bring in a bench so he and his wife could sit out in the evenings and enjoy the garden while the sun set. The more he thought about it, the better he liked the idea.

When they were kids, he and James had spent summers with their grandfather who had a gift for making things grow. Harold remembered him as a bent-shouldered old man, wearing a straw hat with a drooping rim so wide it covered his eyes and flapped loosely over the bridge of his nose. Every morning, they'd work in the garden, squishing fat, green tomato worms or lugging a bushel basket along the rows while their grandfather filled it with vegetables. Back then, James wasn't the pale listless boy he later became, endlessly begging him to play war games. He had strong legs and a square body. The sun had favored the red tints in his hair and turned his face so tan that his eyes looked like the blue marbles in the Chinese checkers set. Harold wondered if they still sold bushel baskets like the ones his grandfather had. If they did, he'd be sure to buy a couple. Just for old time's sake.

"What, and track more mud into the house?" his wife had said in response to his vegetable garden idea. "Don't I have enough to do around here without that?"

"I just thought ..."

"Loretta Blake's husband builds bird houses and sells them at the farmer's market. Why can't you do something useful? Like build bird houses." She was taking the stuff from the dryer. He watched her bending stiff-legged over the laundry basket, folding his undershirts and matching his socks. The softened muscles in her upper arms jiggled as she snapped out the wrinkles in the dishtowels. "And that bathroom door still doesn't shut right," she reminded him.

"I'll check the hinges." But instead of looking at the broken door, he went to the guest room. The army was as he left it, standing, waiting, hoping for action. He wished his brother was here so instead of begging off, he could sit on the edge of the bed, and say something like, "let's have at it."

James' eyes would light up like the big blue *Whoa Daddies* firecrackers their father set off on the Fourth. He would have taken the lead, pushing his men forward, rolling marbles to knock over Harold's advancing army, and making pow-pow noises. He would have wanted to win, of course, and Harold would have let him. After all, he was older and winning wouldn't have meant as much to him.

Harold walked to the window and looked down on the completed trenching job in the back yard. The grass would soon be taking hold and covering the bare earth along the sewer line. Raised vegetable beds was a good idea, but his wife wasn't seeing it that way. He could go ahead and build them, but without her approval, his heart wasn't in it. He wanted her with him. Like the old days. When they were together. But now, she didn't want him. She wanted someone like Loretta's husband who built birdhouses. He ran his hand through his thinning hair, ruffling it a bit to cover the encroaching bald spots that were leaving a kind of widow's peak at the center of his forehead.

What had happened? Were there times when his wife, like James, had reached out to him but he found excuses to avoid her? Too busy at work. Preoccupied by deadlines. Looking elsewhere for approbation. Now, when he came close, she turned away, her broad bulwark of a backside standing between him and any overtures he tried to make, the tone of her voice a wall against which his words had no leverage. No particular incident marked the beginning of their estrangement, but like James's life, his marriage had slipped away and he barely noticed until it was gone.

He took an empty shoebox from the closet, dusted the cover, carefully wrapped the army men in tissue paper, and packed them away. No reason for playing games now. Or planning a trip to Hawaii, for that matter. Once the opportunity to engage passed, it didn't return. He could see it now; he had been missing in action for too long. He was storing the box in the back of the top shelf when he heard his wife's voice.

"What are you doing up there so long?"

Her voice whipped up the stairwell like an unbidden gust of winter wind. It jangled his nerves. He glanced around to make sure nothing in the room was amiss, straightened his grandmother's quilt, and closed the guest room door. He lingered, enjoying the sudden quiet, then descended the stairs, ready to face whatever he had done wrong that day.

May as well work 16 hours a day, can't go home anyway

Nancy Carol Moody

December 9, 1966

Sweets, The Navy won't let us say where we are. The Marines hit the beach at 0400. Don't expect me stateside anytime soon. I'll never get a hot shower. Did you find out what it'll cost to fix the car? It's not paid for until June and I don't want it wrecked again before then. Last night we were in a storm. The inside of the ship was a shambles. You'd told me already about the squirrel. I hate to see Mel Jr get attached to the thing. It's only going to chew up the woodwork trying to get out. Oh well maybe the cat will eat it. Must finish this fast. A helo's coming in 5 minutes. Tell Cindy Daddy loves her. You be careful.

>   the harbor under fog
>   an envelope
>   held to light

Bruised Path

Jeremy Schnee

A fight is not won by one punch or kick. Either learn to endure or hire a bodyguard.—Bruce Lee

When I went home from the martial arts school, the skin on my ribs was so sensitive that untying my *gi*, my uniform, felt like peeling tape from my chest. The thick white cotton scraped away and when the shirt opened, a bruise the size of a baseball covered my ribs. Dark as a tattoo, gray and yellow surrounded the outer edge. In the center, two blue divots marked the imprint of knuckles. It hurt to step, twist, and even to breathe. I wasn't sure if my ribs were broken, wasn't sure if I needed a hospital, but I definitely knew at age seventeen, I was far too old to be bullied.

In part, I started studying karate because I'd always been smaller than average. In elementary school, I occasionally hid on the fringes of a playground to avoid a bigger and tougher kid who I'd been unlucky enough to irritate during recess. In junior high, I talked, joked, or flattered my way out of a few fights. Freshman year of high school, I did my best to dodge that typical jerk senior who got such a thrill out of pushing us much younger teenagers around. I figured everyone got picked on at some point. Sometimes it came to a scuffle, most times it didn't. As the years passed, I thought I'd outgrown all that. I was about to graduate high school. I could drive. I had a job. I was becoming a man.

When we sparred in karate class, or *kumite*, the Japanese word used in the dojo/school, the idea wasn't to hurt each other. We wore pads like squashed pillows on our fists and ankles; however, exercising control protected more than this gear. Pulling a punch or kick at the last second was something any of us who'd been practicing a few years could do. I could punch at a wall full force and stop within half an inch.

We were also supposed to be classmates, learning the same lessons and helping each other improve. That was how I saw it. The bruise on me was intentional. Something Chris had laughed about.

"Little too much for you," he said after we finished sparring.

Like bloodying my nose a few weeks before, this was no accident. Neither were the jokes he made when he called me Shorty or said

Stridex was cheap and plentiful. He was a student at the school before I started. At twenty-four, he had seven years on me and was one rank higher. Whereas I was a brown belt, he had a black stripe across his and was just one step away from his Shodan—a title to most practitioners far more important than the commercially associated black belt that comes with it.

Little too much. The words echoed in my head when we lined up after sparring for the end of class. They echoed as we bowed, as I retreated to the locker room, grabbed my bag and, not saying a word to anyone, almost ran from the dojo.

At least with the raining shower, I knew my family wouldn't hear me wincing as drops pelted the bruise. Lying flat on my back that night, not sleeping, my breath wheezing, I wondered more and more whether I should go to the hospital. If it looked like I'd been hit with a sledgehammer on the surface, I wondered what kind of internal damage there might be. If my parents found out, I was afraid they'd think I shouldn't train at the dojo anymore. Or worse, I was afraid they'd try to get involved in the matter.

Chris wasn't that much bigger, a couple inches taller. He was thin and lanky, strong though. I'd seen him punch through three slabs of cement once. When he attacked, the muscles in his chest looked like a braid of ropes.

I didn't consider myself lackluster either. Since the first martial arts class I'd taken three years prior, I practiced every day. I could stand on my hands and do push-ups. We had what looked like a giant clothes hanger hooked from the ceiling in the dojo and I could dangle from this like a bat to do sit-ups. I started the day with jumping jacks and every night after school I trained at least an hour, mainly doing repetitions of basic strikes, blocks, and kicks of Goju-Ryu style. My old karate teacher said in order to punch like a bullet, block when my eyes were closed, and have rooted balance for kicking, I needed to do each movement one hundred thousand times and maybe then I'd start to have decent technique. So I did practice. But Chris was still bigger, stronger, and better than me.

I hadn't always trained at the same school as him. I'd been Sensei Bridenbaugh's last student. He was a patient and wise teacher, and even had the honor to train in Okinawa when he was young. Though Caucasian, the master instructors respected him enough that he both trained and taught in their dojos. In his late sixties, his body was beginning to give. On cold days he could barely make a fist. During class his ankles ballooned and he often rubbed his hips. His technique was powerful, but when he tried to punch or kick he couldn't hide the pain. His legs waivered in stances and, to prospective students, he must have looked like an old cripple. So other students stopped joining until I was the last.

In an empty dojo, there was too much echo on the wood floor, too much open air between brick walls. I knew it was a burden on him to drive out and dress in his gi. Before retiring, he wanted to ensure I kept training and suggested the new school: The Shin-Suiy-Kan Dojo. My new instructor, Sensei Jacobs, was in his late twenties. Still learning himself, he already had many students.

My best guess why Chris resented me was because I came to the dojo almost the same rank as him. Most martial arts classes line up with the highest ranking students to the right of the room and descending left. At the beginning and end of class, we stood close enough to hear one another breathe. None of the lower ranked students resented me. When they bowed to me, their eyes went to the floor. White and yellow belts in class even called me, "sir," when Sensei Jacobs asked me to teach them a *kata*—a choreographed set of moves designed to teach students to move in different stances, blocking, striking, and kicking.

By the next morning, the bruise had sunk deeper into the skin and muscle on my ribs. Walking the halls at school, I made sure not to carry books in my right hand. I was careful not to bump into desks and careful in lunch lines. Even eating, it stung. I definitely didn't practice in my garage as usual. Instead of going to karate class, I got a stomachache. This was what I told my parents.

"Really?" they said. I missed Tuesday's class and then Thursday's and they started to question what was wrong.

"Something I ate," I swore.

Even Sensei Jacobs called me. I'd never missed a class in the three months since I started at the new dojo. I came to highly respect him after transferring. He placed first in local tournaments, actually had a small room full of trophies. He could move like a rabbit and kick like a horse, people said. Not only that, he respected me and respected my former training, said he was glad to have me as his student.

I told him my stomach was bugging me. He didn't know of the problem I had with Chris. The visible injuries, bloody nose, a few times when I limped from a kick to the leg, looked close enough to accidents. Chris was one of Sensei Jacob's first students. He was often relied on to demonstrate and other classmates talked about what a good guy he was. Were I to have told Sensei Jacobs, I wasn't sure he'd believe me. And I didn't know how to tell him what had happened without sounding like I was weak—like a wimp.

"I should be back soon," I said.

A few days passed, tenderness lessened, color faded from the outer edge. I still found it hard to sleep or do much of anything. In my immobility, I fantasized about smashing the big nostrils of Chris's nose like a peanut. I pictured kneeing his ribs, throwing him in joint locks and twisting until tendons snapped. I wanted him to cry out in pain and even better, fear.

When I trained with Sensei Bridenbaugh, I didn't learn much about fighting. In three years we never sparred more than five times total. His philosophy was that mastering basics, repeating katas, and understanding meaning behind moves was enough to prepare us for a fight should we one day need it. He always said, "You need to get to know yourself, know what you are capable of and respect the journey. If every day you are slightly better at martial arts than the day before, then you are on the right path. Be like a tree and grow."

Bullshit. I resented the three years I wasted training with him. The reason I signed up for martial arts in the first place was to learn to defend myself. To a degree, I could hold my own when we sparred. My stances were solid. My blocks timed right. But there was learning to close the gap, recognizing fake-outs, spotting a telegraph, off-balancing an opponent. There was just learning to spar without always backing away. My training lacked some fighting practicality for sure, but I didn't just want to be able to defend myself. I wanted to beat the shit out of Chris or anyone like him who came into my life.

Of course, another option was never going back to the dojo. However, at age seventeen, I had never been to a party, not a party without parents, with loud music and drinking. I never went out on weekends. Actually, I didn't have many friends, definitely not a girlfriend. As for school, I wasn't involved with clubs or associations. I had never played sports, never gone to a dance. My grades were somewhere between average and scraping by. I worked somewhat on weekends, though I wasn't saving for any sort of well-planned future. It was a part-time fast-food job. So it was not like martial arts provided a social life. It was not like it provided an excuse for poor grades, for going through high school with little in the way of experience. Martial arts was the one good thing I did. I didn't just like it. When the muscles in my arms and legs felt ten times too heavy, when my heart beat so fast my rib cage shook, when I dodged a kick by an inch, made fists so tight my knuckles turned white, I loved it. And though I didn't know what lay ahead in the future, I someday hoped I'd train long enough to run my own dojo. So I had to go back.

A week later the bruise still hurt when I touched it, burned when I twisted for a kick or punch, but I was ready to train again. I doubted Chris knew why I missed class the past week. He didn't as much as look at me when I returned. That was fine. More than anything I wanted to avoid him. Every time Sensei announced what we'd do next, my stom-

Jeremy Schnee

ach swirled. Luck seemed on my side when we didn't spar.

That good luck or maybe just coincidence—I suppose I'd eventually call it opportunity—wasn't yet to end. As we lined up before leaving, Sensei made an announcement. Chris wouldn't be around for a while. For the next two months he was going to Illinois for job training. I couldn't hide smiling as I bowed. Coming back to class specifically that night was perfect then. Except as I left the dojo, I thought about two months from now. Surely while away he'd still practice. I knew what I had to do then too.

Starting the next day, I woke hours before school started. I dusted off an old fitness bench in the garage and began the day lifting weights, hoping to push my muscles beyond the daily push-up and sit-up routine. Which I still did, as well as jumping rope until my ankles trembled. All day at school, I looked forward to going to the dojo. On nights we didn't have class it was empty. Sensei trusted me with a key to open the door for other students in case he was late, or since I was an upper rank, to train on my own.

I hung a heavy bag from the chains in the ceiling. Full of foam and sand, it felt like cement. When we hit the bag in class, we wore punching gloves or ankle guards. I didn't bother. My attacks clapped through the dojo as the bag swayed and buckled. For hours I hit it as hard as I could. When I left, my knuckles were bleeding and my shins purple. It didn't matter. The next day everything hurt worse, but I was learning to push through pain. The worst, anyway, was still fading black to blue on my ribs.

I decided to no longer practice katas or any aspect of martial arts that didn't relate to fighting. After bag-training, I moved across the floor in fighting stances, back and forth against imaginary opponents. If I got tired, if my lungs felt ready to pop or my muscles cramped, I simply thought of Chris and pushed harder. Sometimes after training I could barely walk. Although after a few weeks, my calloused knuckles no longer bled and my shins no longer swelled. Soon I even began riding my bike the three miles to the dojo. After training I'd push to ride home as fast as I could. Eventually, I didn't get tired and took longer routes.

Students at the dojo noticed a change. They noticed during warm-ups, I wasn't breathing as hard as I used to. They noticed when I punched or kicked, my gi whipped and the snapping cotton was heard all around the room. From week to week, I felt faster and stronger. During all my training I could never see my own face. When I'd spar with someone, which I often requested we do, they said my eyes burned red. Like a light switch, I turned to looking mean. I took this as a compliment. Sensei Jacobs even noticed. He used to have to take it easy on me.

Soon I could block most of his attacks and sometimes hit him with a punch to the chest or even tap my heel on his head.

A few other things happened during this time. Namely, I graduated high school. My parents threw a party and everyone there—mainly relatives—asked what I would do next. I didn't know. My parents had gotten catalogs from local colleges. I didn't even look through them. I had picked up extra hours at work and full-time was a possibility in my future, although ultimately these other things didn't matter. Graduating meant I had more time to train. At home, if I wasn't in the garage lifting weights, I was eating or sleeping. I barely saw my parents or the rest of my family. The dojo became a second home. Even Sensei joked about setting up a cot so I could just sleep there.

Summer went on. I never once wavered in my dedication. I gained a few pounds of muscle. From all the punching, veins stood out on my shoulder like branches of blue yarn. My legs, even when not flexing, felt solid as tree trunks. Sure I looked stronger, but my appearance didn't convey the greatest accomplishment I felt regarding the training. Near the end of the two months, Sensei came in the dojo and asked about all the grit on the floor. I hadn't noticed, but the heavy bag had begun to rip at the seams, pebbles and sand leaking out when I hit it.

The bruise healed too. Over those first weeks it faded from purple to pink and eventually disappeared. I still looked for it often. I still thought about Chris, and soon the night came when he would return. I showed up early. All the other students were looking forward to seeing him. I was stretching on the edge of the dojo when he walked in. There was some commotion as others greeted him, and said how great it was to have him back. After he came out of the locker room in his gi, I just nodded.

"I hear you've been training a lot," he said. In the joy of reuniting with everyone else, he seemed to have had me confused with someone else.

"Practicing a little more," I said, "You?"

"Outside work, there wasn't a lot to do in Illinois besides practice."

Good. The last thing I wanted to hear was that he was rusty. Before class started I requested we spar. Sensei said he'd work it in. We warmed up, did some partner exercise, maybe weapons defense, or grappling, and maybe we did some *katas*. I can't recall exactly and nothing much mattered to me until the end of class when Sensei announced it was time for *kumite*. Everyone began to partner off. I stepped in front of Chris, said his name. He nodded and we spread to a corner of the dojo.

"Go easy on me," he joked.

I hadn't yet realized the dynamic was already changing. So far, I suppose in response to my own confidence, he showed me nothing but respect. But this was survival, at least for my place in the dojo. This was revenge. Like a stick on a fence, I rapped my knuckle down the ribs where the bruise had been.

We bowed. We moved to fighting stances—feet loose on the ground, floating almost, and our fists wrapped tight as knots. Sensei yelled, "*Hajime!*" Chris punched, I blocked. I kicked; he dodged. Back and forth, we didn't touch each other those first few seconds. He was strong and fast as ever. Punches seemed to come from nowhere and his kicks shoved me across the floor as I blocked them. I too had speed and power in my corner. A fake to his face almost opened up a punch to the chest and when I charged forward with a flurry of attacks, he did something he never used to; he backed away.

By now he noticed a change in me. Teeth gritting, eyes sharp as knives, he also looked like he wanted to show me, despite all my practice, he was still better. As he rocked forward, I stepped back, blocked his punch and countered with a roundhouse kick—a hook swinging outside in—towards his face. He blocked, slapped my foot toward the floor, intending to throw me off balance, which he did. He rushed forward, cocked his fist to his side. I was not sure how hard he would have hit. Maybe he'd have gone all out, bruised me again. Maybe he would have chuckled, asked if he was too much. However, as my foot hit the floor and my balance buckled, I recovered, faster than he thought me capable, faster actually than I thought myself capable. Bouncing the blocked kick from the floor, I leaned entirely on my back leg and lifted my front. Pulling my knee to my stomach, just as he moved forward with the punch, I thrust like a piston and planted my heel square in his ribs.

With this leg and this sidekick, I'd later snap through four wooden boards. He was entirely open, his momentum moving forward. Most likely, ribs would break. It could have been drastic. It could have been everything I wanted. As sweat gleamed down my forehead, as my breath puffed with exertion, as I felt my leg driving forward and his body giving way, something else happened.

Over the past two months I had learned to train. I had bettered myself. Sure there was anger. Pain was consistent fuel. But that didn't mean I had to hurt Chris. Did he deserve it? Possibly. Did that make it right? Probably not. But this wasn't the reason I hesitated with the kick just as it connected.

Maybe in that moment I was beginning to understand Sensei Bridenbaugh, the things he said about the journey and constantly growing. I was beginning to understand what he meant about not just knowing the moves, but the intentions behind them. As for my own life, I think I even realized that for once I was good, genuinely good at something. Such a thought could help me continue to train in years ahead, to get my Shodan and even if I didn't always train in martial arts, maybe the lessons I learned could apply to other things: asking a girl out, going to college, setting off on my own, anything I was afraid of, really.

The past few months, sore muscles, aching joints, beat-up knuckles, the countless hours in the dojo, it couldn't all be about Chris. I knew even then it had to be about more. So I pulled the full force of the kick.

Still, when my heel connected, Chris grunted and teetered back. Winded, he coughed. His face turned pink. He attacked angry, swung without control, signaling attacks with clenches of his face. He tried to grab my gi and throw me. I stood solid and pushed him away. With his sloppy attacks and flimsy stances, I could have hit him again any time. I could have punched him right in the ribs where he was still soft from the kick. Heaving and out of breath, I could have bloodied his nose, or kicked to the sciatic nerve in his leg to watch him limp. But I simply blocked all of his attacks and waited.

"*Yame!*" Sensei Jacobs yelled. We stopped, separated. I didn't say anything like, "Too much." I didn't sneer, didn't smile. I just bowed. He barely nodded and stared off to an empty wall of the dojo. His face was still pink and he couldn't yet catch his breath. I held the bow, just looked him in the eye, and he never met my gaze. Then I walked away and lined up for the end of class. There I stood straight, strong, and confident.

Poem as Artifact

Jamie North

The past lets go in a dream,
and you return to what you
thought you'd forgotten –

The shadow on your shoulder
radicates wings, grows feathers
in a crevasse of blades.

Your hunger for information
turned to exhaustion, the need
to bunker down, close-in the world.

I will build a fortress in a stream,
open small burdens with the heart,
tell you the day will come when

there is an admonition you
need not to hear.

Orville Wright, Meet the B-17 Flying Fortress

B. B. Pirelli

We all have different reasons for joining. Some call it rebellion. Some call it a sport. I call it culture. We were the shambles of normal society, pieced together in a jigsaw of assorted values. At some point, we all chose to pick up a set of wheels and ride. We chose skateboarding to fill a void in our lives, one of the many stoppers available to plug this seeping emptiness of being.

At thirteen years old, I made my own beginning.

"Your turn," Simon said as he slid the deck over to me. Tentatively, I placed a foot on top and shifted my weight over. Before me lay one of the staircases at Nixon Elementary School. Six concrete steps, bound by two rails coated in flaky teal paint. On my first day of kindergarten, Dad had labeled the color as "celeste," in his typical fascination with the meaningless nuances of the world. Behind me was the local gang of skaters, a motley crew of students, each attempting to fill that missing piece in their lives with the adrenaline rush accompanied with successful tricks and near misses.

Mounting the board, I pushed all my weight forward and watched the surroundings blur around me. *Thump thump.* Vibrations rattled through my frame as my body cushioned the shock of the wheels forcing themselves over the crags and cracks of the concrete below. *Thump thump.* At the forefront of my vision was the nearing staircase. As I raced toward it, my perception of the world began to narrow in on those very steps. In an instant, I had popped up the board and was airborne, shocked to feel the board still beneath my feet while I shot through the sky.

As I began my descent, I already knew what would happen. Momentum was shackling me downward, and there was no way I could land. As the board touched the ground, I shot out behind it, skidding across the concrete below, and ripping through the skin of my exposed elbows and palms. For a moment, I lay there in shock before I forced myself to my feet. The skaters erupted in cheers. I had dueled gravity for a moment, feeling more like one of the Wright Brothers than myself. It was art; it was freeing.

Instantly, I was hooked.

Long before, my parents had walked me along the sidewalks of downtown Palo Alto, where we avoided skateboarders at all costs. Surly and abusive, they would sink to casting insults and curses at a child walking past. Terror.

So imagine how stoked my parents were when they found my first skateboard deck beneath a sweaty jacket in my room. A lecture came first. I saw tears forming in Mom's eyes. They told me I couldn't ride. A week later their futility was apparent—I came home from "school" covered in bruises from a failed trick. They pleaded with me, letting desperation unveil itself behind their tightly wound facades. Finally, we settled on kneepads and a helmet. I wore them for two weeks before I "lost" them at the skate park.

I understood why they hated skateboarders so much. They are the poster children of teenage problems, criminals in training. A simple scan over YouTube will unveil the horrors that they commit: boards swung at cops' heads, trashed property, broken limbs of bystanders. But I would never have been one of them. "Stereotypes," I had said, "not every skateboarder is bad." They still tried to keep me from it. They reminded me of my future.

I never really thought too much about college except for when my parents brought it up. It was always kind of a given that I would end up there. We had the money—at least for a state school. Somehow I had managed to float by with B's in my classes. As a freshman in high school, Harvard might not have been on the horizon, but I was going somewhere for sure. Most likely to a Cal State, maybe to a UC, but I was going to go; it was certain. My philosophy was that it didn't matter if I tried in high school, just so long as I tried in college. From there I could worry about the future—but for now, I was just in it for the ride.

Three months since my first stair set, we were back at Nixon once again, standing before the same steps that had sent me sprawling backward. I had spent the months in my carport, practicing ollies and kickflips for hours on end, riding and falling, forming a collection of scars and scrapes across my elbows and knees, discoloration worn with pride. YouTube instructional videos and determination were all I needed to impel my desire of a successful landing. I'll admit I was a little nervous, but knowing that skinned elbows were the worst that awaited a failed attempt, I mounted my board once more and began pushing toward the stairs.

As I glided toward the stairs, the *thump thump* wasn't there any-more. I had long become inured to the sound of wheels fighting across rough ground. No, all I could see was the set of stairs in front of me. Pushing the tail of the board to the ground, and then suddenly jump-ing outright, I lifted the board and myself well into the air. Gracefully, I soared upward, the board feeling like another appendage of my body, grafted straight to my feet.

I landed, letting the wheels clatter to the ground as I pressed my weight down fully. I rolled smoothly away.

I watched the video on Simon's phone later that evening. The gentle arc through the air, the fluid movements—they were beautiful in their own way. Why do most people call dancing art, but not skateboarding?

Over time, Simon became the leader of our group, and I liked to think of myself as his right-hand man. He stood at five feet, eleven inches tall, a gangly, awkward height. His nose had a suspicious lopsided crook, as if it had been broken at least once before. But for some reason, he was so damn likable—he could talk you into anything and himself out of anything.

Fueled by Rice Krispy Treats and Linkin Park, we roamed the city, turning wreckage into wonder, stray pipes into seamless playgrounds. That's where the magnificence of skateboarding was. Turning the blight that marks an urban landscape into beauty. Jagged steps were a place where art could be made, not just a crack in the city's budget. Construc-tion sites became targets for our high-speed artwork.

It was a simple idea really, very simple. The decay and filth that made up our lives could be turned into artwork. But for some reason, society could never grasp it the same way. They would chase us from our findings, throwing stones and calling threats upon us. And like rats, we would scamper away. Why couldn't they see that we were the good ones, that not all skateboarders were bad? We could make our art with-out harming anyone else, and that was all we would do. Hell, we were making beauty—why weren't they appreciating it?

I'm not sure when stairs weren't enough anymore, but at some point the meager teaspoon of adrenaline from a short liftoff and descent couldn't satisfy me. Our art deserved a larger scale.

I placed my board in the gutter of some store's rooftop, and wrapped my fingers around the thin aluminum outcropping. I could feel it give slightly as I let more of my weight hang from it. With one awkward motion I pulled my weight upward, feeling my body shake from the exertion. The gutter began to hang lower and lower, but I still heaved my body upward, throwing my leg on top of the gravelly surface above.

B. B. Pirelli

The gutter sunk lower once more, this time letting off a metallic groan against the force of my mass. I scrambled up onto the rooftop just as a visible dent formed in the gutter below.

Having scaled the roof first, it was now my job to help the rest of the group. I lay on the edge, extending a hand down to Simon below. With one hand on the now-deformed gutter and one hand in mine, I pulled him upward until his torso rested against the rough rooftop as well. Simon flashed me a goofy grin. "Thanks, man."

Gapping was our game now. With a running start, we rode as fast as we could toward the edge of the roof, focusing only on the rooftop of the neighboring building, displaced by what must have been a six-foot alleyway. Spanning that gap was our goal.

The adrenaline pumped through my body once more. We risked more than a few layers of skin now—we risked broken bones and trespassing charges as we neared the massive crevice that marked the intersection between the two buildings. Our speed picked up, and the wind funneled around me, sending particles of dirt and debris shooting straight into my face. I futilely tried to squint my eyes until a fleck of gravel lodged itself into my eyelid. I shut my eyes entirely—I was going in blind, as the board progressed to the edge.

I felt the support of the roof vanish beneath me as I lifted off. Was I going fast enough? I opened my right eye and glanced downward to see the distant alleyway beneath me, and I froze. My balance on a tiny board suspended in the air was all that kept me from plummeting to-ward the ground below. In front of me was the ever-approaching roof-top. It was absolutely beautiful, another chapter in our vendetta against gravity, two teens floating above the collective filth of downtown.

I won't say that the landing was perfect, but the board definitely touched down on the other side before launching me forward as one of the wheels got caught on a piece of gravel. I rolled to a halt on the rooftop and picked myself up.

Simon had better luck with his landing; he was still upright, but slightly shaken. He reached into his back pocket and pulled out a ciga-rette, lighting it up on the spot and taking a drag. He began to sputter and cough on the smoke, wheezing fumes out of his partially opened mouth. I had never seen him smoke before. Was this his first time? He silently motioned the pack toward me, and with a trembling hand I took one from the pack and placed it between my lips. With a flick of the lighter, my cigarette was lit and I sucked down the smoke.

It was thrilling to have smoke fill my lungs. Disgusting, yes, but thrilling all the while. A tiny adrenaline rush followed as I thought of all the statistics about smoking deaths—I was toying with danger once again, and I loved it.

Sprinting down an alleyway, skateboards under our arms, we ran as fast as we could. The red and blue beacon of a police car cut through the night in the distance. "Don't run," droned a voice through the car's loudspeaker, but there was no chance of us heeding the request—we vanished into the night.

Minutes before, we had been riding downtown, grinding on rails, and trying to find thrills wherever we could. Skating just wasn't a challenge anymore. However when the cop pulled up, we bolted. It felt oddly refreshing to run away, slinking into the night.

Of course, even the action of skateboarding is risky. As much as I try to glorify our performances, I recognize that they can be branded as a variety of crimes, from disturbing the peace to vandalism. An unjust depiction, maybe, but those are the rules the police play by. They set the rules, and we learned to game our way through them.

The easiest game of all is running. We've got wheels and youth on our side—so we use them. Imagine a big ol' porker of a police officer, loaded down with a belly from his driving all day, fumbling his way out of his car. He doesn't stand a chance—we can recede into the shadows, gutters and alleyways before he's even pulled his key from the ignition. Sometimes though, they can take you by surprise—but that's where the fun begins, when you find yourself sprinting through yards, over fences, and through obstacles.

Months later, Simon and I sat in front of a Walgreens, smoking away. I wouldn't call it a new habit at all. After I realized that any semblance of danger only came from years of abuse, the thrill subsided once more.

The thrill was gone from nearly everything now. In the little city of Palo Alto, we must have skated every imaginable spot: construction sites, staircases, even parking garages. We were outgrowing the town—and no matter how many variations we could come up with, skateboarding wasn't as dangerous as it once seemed. We weren't living on the edge anymore. There were so many ways we could play with death—grinds along railway tracks, leaping from building to building—but they were all the same now, novel at first, but only fading into the gloriously inane.

"Let's go break some shit," Simon said.

Simon handed me the bottle of spray paint silently, putting a finger to his lips. "Real fucking simple. Just write something on that stop sign up there, and get out. Make it funny too. None of that pussy shit."

It was simple enough. The only semblance of order in the decrepit parking lot was the bright red stop sign. A single streetlight illuminated our sign in the dark night. The lot lay desolate, except for an old red minivan gathering dust in the far corner of the lot. We had picked this spot because of the "No Skateboarding" sign planted clearly on the entrance, our siren call to action.

I snatched the spray paint from his hand, and started to sprint toward the stop sign. *Thump thump.* I could feel my heartbeat, pulsing away in my forehead. The world around me began to blur, and all I could see centered in front of me was the bright red stop sign.

Thump thump. As I neared the sign, I began shaking the can of spray paint in my hand as I ran, hearing the sound of metal on metal as pressure built up within. *Thump thump.* I reached the sign, and with an elegant scrawl, I formed the words "don't" and "believin'," above and beneath the bold letters. *Don't Stop Believin'.* Classic stop sign graffiti. Everybody loves Journey.

Thump thump. I knew something was wrong. Why was I still so tense? It was then that I noticed the light. The minivan's headlights were on all of a sudden, and it looked like it was moving. *Thump thump. Thump thump. Thump thump.*

I tried running. But there's nowhere you can hide in an empty parking lot. If there were cars somewhere, maybe I could have rolled under one, maybe I could have slunk away. But no—the van was coming at me now. There was no escape.

I winced as I heard the squeal of tires. The car drifted in a curve around me, the hideous stench of hot rubber filling the air as the door slid open and a burly man clad in black rushed out. "Police. Don't move." I caught a glimpse of his badge. It looked real enough, and I froze.

He placed a hand on my shoulder and pushed me down until I was sitting. I faded out of consciousness for a moment. It was a blur—everything was a blur—everything was happening so fast—life was happening so fucking fast, and all I knew was that in that one moment, I had thrown away college. I had thrown away my future.

There's something absolutely terrifying about being arrested when you know that you actually did something wrong. There's a real sense of fear there, and you know that the damn cop can sense it. A churning forms in your stomach and you know that you messed up. You know that there's no going back, there's no undoing what you did. Try as you might, you're going down right now, and there's no escape. *Law & Order* never did getting arrested any sort of justice. There's no witty line as the police officer shoves you into the backseat, handcuffs wrapped tightly around your wrists, nearly cutting off your circulation. You only get silence in the ride to the police station.

And then it's over. Your parents come to pick you up, and they're just as disgusted with you as you are with yourself. You relive your own feelings as they repeat to you over and over again, what you already know—you've messed up, there's no going back. Some things are irreversible.

But the worst part is what they don't say, what you're hoping to God they don't even realize. It hangs in the back of your mind all the while as you try to think of the responses you would make. But they don't need to say it. The truth is in your head already, ricocheting throughout your skull, unrelentingly driving its point home: your freedom lies amputated, your art is nothing more than a shitty joke sprayed across a stop sign. Is that beauty?

Amy Miller

Ours is the land
of the valley of the alphabet.
Ours is the bland mouse brown,
the mottled stockings that still
won't trap the eye.
We vanish in the crosswalk,
mindful of the blooming curves
of friends who step
before us and behind.
Never the first called
or the last, ours are the faces
half-turned in the middle row,
the names learned once and forgotten,
the medium ones meandering the halls
of the past, making lists
of those who never knew us,
mincing with the bright blade of memory
the words we might have said.

On Being A Grown Up

Sasha Ives

On the night of my eighteenth birthday, after a dinner out with my parents, I had my best friends pick me up at home and, on the way to our favorite hang out spot on the piers of West Wharf Beach, we pulled up to the nearest gas station snack-mart so I could consummate my initiation into the adult world. They followed me inside where I proudly walked up to the counter.

"Sir," I started as the other girls went to pick out snacks. The cashier was another young adult who had graduated in the class above us. "I'll take the longest, fattest cigar you've got. And while you're at it, throw in a lotto ticket. And a pack of Marlboro Red 100's."

I looked around the counter to see Naomi in the chip aisle, shaking her head with a tisk-tisk.

"Anything else?"

I thought for a moment, then decided it wasn't very grown-up-like to be indecisive at the counter.

"That should do it," I said. Paid. Waited for the three of them to check out before walking back to the car. I didn't even have to show my ID.

I sat shotgun, thinking to myself through the gleam of the moonlit night that distortedly reflected itself through the fingerprints on the passenger window of Kerry's Jeep that something was missing. Lotto, cigar, cigarettes ... There must have been something else, something new to which on that day I finally had constant, life changing, perfectly legal access. Maybe it was something I couldn't buy at a gas station.

I thought about it a bit more; pondered the potential of having the right to vote and consequently decided that the opportunity to use it arises too infrequently to truly celebrate. It couldn't be pornography either (I was pretty sure you didn't have to be eighteen to find that kind of thing on the Internet).

Looking back now, at almost twenty-three, I guess that's about all that eighteen ever was: an entire lifetime of build-up for lotto tickets and the start of a slow suicide by tobacco products. No grand rite of passage, no sudden transformation at midnight into everything I'd ever hoped I'd be. All those years spent dreaming, playing "family" with the little girls in the neighborhood, and demanding that I play the older sister (popular, Barbie-beautiful high-school diva, deservedly snobby and specifically, eighteen). If only I could've known in childhood what I would've known not so long after (I would've made a lot more friends on the playground).

What I really wanted from adulthood wasn't an inalienable right, or something I could get with money, or for free online. There's a certain respect I expected at eighteen that comes with being a grown-up: an understanding of where one fits into society. When kids start seeing you as "missus" instead of as "that kid," for example. When your parents and teachers and bosses start talking to you like you're a peer instead of trying to mold and shape you like you're a piece of play dough, until you're just how they like you, and reprimand you when you burst out from the gaps in the grip of their firmly clasped fingers.

Wanting that and knowing it will take a lot of the wind out of turning twenty-one. I say that from experience. Any average anybody who's been there was probably still looking for freedom the day after their twenty-first birthday; not just from the swirling confines of the Porcelain God, but from adolescent life as a whole.

College has to be where it really starts though, doesn't it? If you're the college type. That's when we begin to realize the flavor of being a grown up, having been forced to take our first baby steps into the real world. We end up maybe hours, even thousands of miles beyond our parents' reach. We start inventing our own schedules and study hours. Sleep all day, stay up all night just because no one's there to say "no."

Professors are a lot different than grade school teachers, too. In almost every way. Most importantly, they don't slap you on the knuckles with a ruler for being you.

Heck, you might even have to work a full-time job in college just to stay in school and pay for your first and very own apartment. You might have to learn to cook something other than buttered noodles and microwave dinners for the sake of your own sanity. Work, study, bring home the bacon, pay the bills, sleep, repeat. Get your degree and get a better job. And maybe you repeat that too. What's more grown-up than that?

The truth is, at my ripe young age, that's the best I've got. And I have done or am doing almost all of those exceptionally grown up things this very day and what I don't get is why there's still something missing.

No. I don't get micromanaged at work like I did six years ago, and my parents talk with me on the phone often about what I'm doing, but rarely, about how I should do it (unless I'm desperate for their input). The trust, the respect inherent in true adulthood is slowly falling within my reach; and yet, it's still not good enough.

Once in a while, and inevitably so, some aspect of society will cast my nearly grown-up self and me through the deepest levels of self-doubt and maybe that's the problem. For example, I was carded not long ago while buying a rated "M" video game for my brother's birthday at E.B. Games. The cashier looked down at me smugly over his pimpled cheeks and squinted lids and asked, "Can I see your ID, please," and in that moment I was rebirthed in eighteen. Actually, it wasn't even that good, because you only have to be seventeen to legally purchase a rated M video game. As an "adult" individual who lacks confidence in my "grown-up" self, it takes me a few days, even weeks, to fully psychologically recover from an episode such as this; weeks of work, learn, study, earn, pay, sleep, repeat to build myself back up to a point where I can start reaping some vague benefit of adulthood once more.

Even without degrading experiences such as my most recent jaunt to EB Games, college life is draining, and as such, often acts as a kind of devil's advocate to my sense of self-worth. Let me be frank: it is just a lot of work. Especially if you're really giving it a good shot. So much work in fact, especially on top of other jobs, internships, and extracurriculars, I find it almost impossible to believe that any self-respecting adult would stand for this kind of a lifestyle indefinitely. Being a grown-up must therefore mean finding some form of stability in life. Consistency. Regularity. Maybe it just means I'll stop complaining about my privileged life as a white, American female.

When I think of being a grown-up (truly), I think of how badly I want that: that clear cut, regular, consistent day-to-day life. I think maybe that's all I want. I think that right now, life's getting simpler and more complicated at the same time; and maybe I'll be on this train for a while. Until I get there.

But there isn't even really new; can't be, because it doesn't seem nearly as unfamiliar as it should. I realize what I'm thinking of is childhood; when none of the things I'm working toward were any of my concern and I thought the simplest things were complicated and the most complicated were so simple. Maybe I've spent twenty-three years trying to be a grown up when all I've really wanted was to revert back to diaper days. Can't be ...

Time to call my parents.

I sit on a secluded curb as I find and dial the number.

"Iiit's Sasha!" Dad answers first.

"Hey, Pops, what's shakin'?"

He is fifty-four years old and says he worked for ten hours today, and (keeping up the excitement in his voice) that Mom made a fantastic dinner, that his arthritis is kicking in with the slow awakening of another East Coast Winter, but it's not so bad. And now it's time to kick his feet up on the couch and wait for Mommy to go to bed so that he can put on "The Last Word" with Lawrence O'Donnell. As the thought of my day on the other side of the country being less than half over sneaks into the forefront of my brain, I think that sounds nice.

"I'm getting old, Honey," he says, chuckling a bit. "How are YOU?"

I pause for a second. Listening to the slight static that fills up the 3000 miles of physical distance between his cell phone and mine and trying to choke back the shame of thinking about how he's fifty-four years old, working seventy hours a week of manual labor and he sounds better than I do on a Wednesday.

"I want to be old too, Dad" I say playfully, laughing a bit but not really joking, "I want to be just like you."

I want to really look at the facts of aging. I don't think that aging means we change as much as we like to think we do as we get older (if my Dad's any example, though he might very well be the exception). We don't really change that much when crossing bridges between stages of life. Rather, I think being a grown up is a learned skill. In many respects, I think we probably all stay kids forever (though some are less ashamed than others to admit it), use life to blow up our grown-up life-jackets until they're big enough to keep our heads above water, and then tear them off like shedding skin. My dad did that. He doesn't need anything or anybody to keep him going. He just goes. Goes and floats his way. Confidence of craft is the ability to swim instead of struggle. To see everything in its most simple and most complicated terms. To laugh, and to swim.

He laughs too. "Well, I'll tell you this much. I don't care what they say; it doesn't hurt. I promise."

Stopover In Austin

Pat Phillips West

One thumb hooked in the waistband of my jeans,
I look at the bartender with a seductive
smile from under my brand-new cowgirl hat.
He stretches a hand across the bar, says the name's

Jake, asks where I come from. *PBR and bad drugs,
I reply, born at Woodstock the Sunday it rained.
Mom said her labor started while sliding
naked in the mud.*

I slip off the hat, shake out my long, red hair. Sip
my Tallboy, watch as Jake blends foxtrot steps
and line dancing moves while mixing a diabolical
margarita with small red chili pepper slices.

He catches me checking his butt in the back-bar mirror,
winks. Customers share their latest news, one asks for advice.
Like a gypsy king, Jake pulls out a Tarot deck, *Let's see
what the cards have to say.*

My second beer, I'm ready for this dark, six-foot stranger
with gunslinger eyes to tell my fortune. He turns over my first
card, *There's no better place to start than the Fool. How close
to danger do you walk?* he asks turning over the Knight

of Wands in reverse. *Ahhh,* a chuckle rumbles deep
in his throat, *there's your answer, fearless.* I stand on the brass
foot rail, lean across, whisper, *I can tell you what comes next
without a deck of cards.*

The Future of Felicity

Amanda Lara

Sometimes you play with a Ouija board after getting off the phone with your mother. You're not sure if it really *does* contact the dead, but you like to spell out *SCREW THAT BITCH* with the planchette and pretend it's a message from your guardian angel. When you fight with Stephen and come home cursing his name, you do a couple shots before pulling out the board, then demand it to help you find a better boyfriend. Occasionally you'll get drunk enough to ask the board real questions like "how am I going to die" or "will I get laid any time soon," but the planchette never moves on its own and you usually black out after the tenth shot of vodka.

Once, you mentioned this hobby to Stephen in passing; he'd nearly choked on a mouthful of Miller Lite.

"That's bad luck," he'd said, concern crinkling his handsome, scruffy face. "You're not supposed to use a Ouija board alone."

But bad luck is your middle name, because you're *trouble*, always have been. You were the girl who took E at prom and who fucked half a fraternity upon entering college. Sometimes you skim through your high school yearbook and pray to God that those days weren't the highlight of your life, because now you're twenty-seven and still bartend for a living (every now and then you pull out your BA in Sociology and just laugh). If you're not at work or screaming at Stephen, you're probably on the phone with your mother. And if you're *not* on the phone with your mother, you're probably with that stupid Ouija board or drinking yourself to death. Odds are, you'll do all these things within the span of a week.

If you and Stephen aren't fighting, he talks about marriage and a condo in Torrance.

"Why Torrance?" you'll ask.

He'll laugh and reply, "It's close to the studio, Babe. My agent would kill me if we moved too far away, and I want to support us."

Stephen likes to call himself an actor. It's sort of true—he's got a running gig on some daytime soap that you pretend to watch, and a few years back he was an extra on *NCIS*. But you want to laugh every time he talks about having a family; there is no way in hell you'd let an infant come into the world with two parents who barely make enough to afford ramen. But Stephen's one of those actors who likes acting for *acting*, not for the fame, which is actually worse because it meant that he would never quit and get a real job. And when you do picture a future with him, you envision skinny children and nicotine gum. Sometimes you're glad the two of you fight so often. Sometimes you cry and dream of a baby with his eyes.

Today you're spelling out your name on the board: *F-E-L-I-C-I-T-Y*. At work, you're Candi with an 'i', because who the hell would want to order a Bloody Mary from a woman who shares a name with their grandmother? Men, you find, are far more willing to tip Candi than Felicity, especially if Candi laughs at all their drunken jokes and leans over the bar with her tits pushed together.

If you and Stephen had a boy, then he would be Stephen Junior. But if you and Stephen had a girl, she wouldn't be a Felicity—the last thing you'd want for your daughter was to be tied to your side of the gene pool in any way, shape, or form. Bad enough she would have a bartending mother and a high-school-dropout father. No, your daughter would have a good name. Something that meant "smart" or "successful" or "one who shall not follow in the footsteps of her dumbass parents."

Angrily, you shove the planchette to the upper right-hand corner of the board: *NO*. No, you shouldn't think about having kids. Washed-up bad girls and D-list actors didn't *get* to have kids. Did you really want to add "screwing up a child's life" to your resume?

"Goddamn it," you mutter, and push a little white pill between your lips, chasing it with gin. Ibuprofen and alcohol. Maybe tonight's the night your liver will finally fail. Maybe not. You like taking chances.

When you were seven, you wanted to be a poet. When you were fourteen you tried to write a novel about an alien falling in love with a dog, then ran out of steam about halfway through. Some kids drew pictures at the edges of their notes—you wrote words. Three-sentence stories above the formula for the circumference of a circle. Names of characters for books you'd never pen. Every once in a while you'd tear off the parts of the paper with your writing on it; you spent the majority of ninth grade with corner-less notebooks.

Then you turned sixteen. Discovered menthol cigarettes and James Dean, *live fast, die young*. It was a miracle you graduated high school; you barely squeaked out a college degree. After a while, people stopped telling you that there was still time to figure things out. Conversations with your mother became less comforting, more condescending. Your friends were getting married, moving to neighborhoods with low crime rates while you poured shots for balding accountants and wished that Stephen wasn't such a dreamer. Cigarettes weren't killing you fast enough. You reached twenty-seven and your heart was still beating.

The only way you write now is with the Ouija board. Granted, most of the time your work consists of mindless rants or baby names or whatever the hell your intoxicated brain comes up with, but it's writing all the same. Take a shot, write. Pop a pill, write. You pen your craft on a Ouija board and drink like a fish. Maybe Hemingway's ghost was pushing the planchette and dispensing the spirits (ha, ha). If Ouija boards really were portals to the afterlife, you would bet Hemingway would love your compositions.

Tonight is no different. You swirl the plastic triangle around the board, lens focused on letters that are beginning to blur together.

S-T-E-P-H-E-N. F-E-L-I-C-I-T-Y. B-A-B-Y.

Through the haze, you smile. You're not sure if a career in writing would have ever panned out, but you like this. In the midst of all of the fighting, fucking and smoking, this is the time when you get to believe in children and Torrance.

A million Christmases ago, when your mother gave you the board, she'd told you it could also be used to predict the future. She'd said that those who have passed no longer have any concept of time or success.

Sometimes you pretend it's not you who's pushing the planchette around, but some spirit or deity or god who knows more about the future than you ever will.

The Grease Pencils of the Cosmonauts

Terry Spohn

When we made love in the afternoon Henry peeked in through
    the dormer window
and rubbed his private parts while he watched.
Each time we ate rice and beans for breakfast
Henry curled up beneath the table and waited for morsels to fall.
When he wasn't changing the songs on the radio
he was wearing thin the elbows on our favorite shirts.
Every day there was more of him, every night more again,
so that when we woke in the mornings the house was filled
with Henry the way the widow's house filled with Henry after the
    funeral,
the way cathedrals were filled with Henry even when no one was there.
Henry rarely spoke, and we strained to hear what little he said.
We often wondered if he was older than the hedonistic paintings
    of Pompeii,
we guessed that he was because most of the time Henry
had the same look of weary resignation coal miners have in
    photographs.

Our friends and neighbors called Henry by other names,
typing one after another while they searched their computers—
fifth cousin Claude, dead in the woods outside Andersonville,
Great Aunt Charlotte, her nightgown engulfed in flames as she ran out
    into the snow,
and everywhere beneath the boulders and mud the dead watching
    one another,
but Henry never answered to any name any of us had given him.
Instead, he circled like a condor in the breeze above the ball game,
or spent the morning fingering women's slacks that hung in rows
    at Goodwill.
In the evening he pretended to be absorbed with tarnishing the
    silverware.
When we asked Henry what his plans were he stared straight into

the moment
the way a cat watches a caged bird and it felt as if we were adrift
in a tiny yellow life raft atop an ocean of garbled noise—
whale songs and chewing, and a steady bubbling from the muck
where everything had already happened and would happen again.

I know what you're thinking.
You're thinking, *why didn't you just throw him out?*
Oh, we talked about it many times over glasses of chianti at the table,
about how much more space we'd have without Henry,
how each bright morning we'd encounter one another in the kitchen
and wonder what it would be like to walk away hand in hand with
    this fellow orphan whose
name we would never know and who we might soon
touch our lips to for the first time, but we just kept breathing together
and the continent continued its easy slide northward and the
    vitamin bottles
and reading glasses and houseplants of our lives together floated
    up around us
like grease pencils around cosmonauts and all the while Henry,
    sitting in the living room clipping
his nails and listening with that little smile parents have
when a child closes her eyes to make a wish.

The Tube Time Slumber Party: Or, How I Didn't Lose My Virginity

Kori Rosset

First let me just tell you how there are **penises** and there are **vaginas** and how these have been nothing but a huge problem for me.

The first **penis** I ever saw was my own.

The first **vagina** I ever saw that wasn't my mother's was when I was two and I walked in on the daycare lady's son who was a registered pedophile jacking off in the bathroom and watching a girl pee. This is my first memory.

The second **vagina** I ever saw was when I was sixteen and I walked in on OG Grant, sitting on the Tube Time toilet with some girl named Natalie sitting on his colorful **penis**, and how she looked at me like she'd been caught and he looked at me like he'd been sainted.

What I'm saying is toilets are weird.

~FLICK THREADS: AUTHENTIC HOLLYWOOD CONSIGNMENT~

Clawing through the red leather *Beat It* jackets, Madonna's *Blond Ambition* cone bras, Han Solo vests, *Clueless* plaid, and *A Clockwork Orange* fedoras, black, until I finally point the hair dyed/skin died "SALES ASSOCIATE" toward the slinky leather one-piece, something you'd be more inclined to put on a horse than a person, and I say, "This. This is the most amazing thing I have ever seen."

'Cause yes, it's used. And yes, some porn star sweated and got wet all over and inside of it, but they'll all think it's hilarious and they'll love me forever. I buy it for twelve bucks.

~THE USUAL~

Math class isn't over, so I sneak back in and draw cakes and candles and *HAPPY BIRTHDAYS* and *16s* and smiley faces all over the box, waiting for the bell. *W8ing 4 duh BELL.* W a i t i n g f o r t h e b e e e e e e e e e e e l l l.

Burst grandly from classroom with dancer's flourish. Meet Logan and Angel in the commons, obligatory man-shakes, how-do-you-dos, lights down on Logan/zoom in/hard focus, statement of plan:

1. *take Angel's mom's Prius*
2. *pick up OG*
3. *go to Maya's*
4. *steal a nug off her brother*
5. *just generally tear shit up, the fucking usual, why do you always ask me this before we do anything, it's not a suit and tie event, just fucking go with it goddamn it, I mean*

o   **SUBJECT A ~ "LOGAN JOYCE":** Logan was three days younger than me. He took me in as part of the "FRESHMAN ADOPTION PROGRAM" 'cause he thought the picture on my t-shirt was funny. It was a topic of continued debate among those who mattered whether or not he could be certified: *hawt*, but there was no questioning the legend of his sexual exploits, the conclusion being: *he was packing heat.* And though none of the boys had ever seen `the thing itself`, they were sure it was monstrous and not to be trifled with.

do you even realize what this is, you son of a bitch? It's a ball crawl full of drunk sluts hungry for **the d** *You hear me, Kori Rosset? You're not allowed to leave this birthday party until you've lost your goddamn stupid virginity. It's bringing us all down. I won't have it.*

1. *take Angel's mom's Prius*

We pile in, me in perpetual back seat, passing a Swisher Sweet. Angel points at my lap, saying, "What's in the box?"

"Gwyneth Paltrow's severed head."

"Nice."

Angel **SLAP!**s his shades on and **PUNCH!**es it 0-to-60 from the curb, quick **SWERVE!** to avoid collision, back up to 60, "Fuck 'da Police" hyper-compressed and **BLAST!**ing raunchy from his cellphone to the car speakers.

o   **SUBJECT B ~ "ANGEL SANCHEZ":** Angel came with Logan as a package deal. His life goal was to get as much sex as possible [SEE: "**vagina**", SEE ALSO: "*just being a* dude"], and his subscription to the emo scene was exclusively to get **it** in with the emo girls, because as everyone knows: *emo girls never say no*. If you asked him his favorite band, he'd say *AFI*. His real favorite band was *Weezer*.

2.   *pick up OG*

OG lets us in at the door 'cause his parents are too busy yelling and throwing shit at each other to hear the doorbell, let alone notice their son stealing a bottle of whiskey, vodka, and Captain Morgan. We sneak back for the door, but Angel's gone missing. We find him in the bedroom playing pocket pool in front of a poster of Angelina Jolie and her lips.

OG sells it to him for ten bucks. They are both happy with this.

o   SUBJECT C ~ "OG GRANT": The first time I "met" OG was in the middle school locker room when he kicked my bent-over ass in front of everyone and it was everything I could do to not melt into a sobbing puddle of pubescent devastation. He was Logan's best friend. He was nothing to look at particularly and had already gone to work on his beer belly, but there was something magical about him that made everyone just really want his **dick** in their mouth. He left school sophomore year for Job Corps and started living half-time on his girlfriend's couch, eating grilled cheese sandwiches, and just generally being cooler than I'll ever be.

We pile back into the Prius, OG in the back seat with me, patented smile/nod, like, "What's up, K-Dawg?"

My social contentment and sense of self-worth, you wonderful Adonis.

~AND THEN WE~

3.   *go to Maya's*

Maya's mom has a boyfriend, but the boys all talk about her like she's single. She hugs Logan as she lets us in and points us to the stairs.

Maya is in her room, sitting close with Tristan on the bed. Stella is sitting on her boyfriend's lap, River Bowman, the last Young Republican on earth, pinning him down into the beanbag chair. Logan shoves his plump lady butt between Maya and Tristan and sits.

o   **SUBJECT D ~ "MAYA TANNER/BIRTHDAY GIRL #1":**
Maya was Logan's girlfriend(?), and the hottest girl anyone
in the room had ever slept with. When I think about her,
I think about how amazing her mouth looked when she
spoke, and how, when she fucked another guy, Logan
said it wasn't a big deal. They didn't have a label. And
how bummed he was when he said that.

We pass out presents:
OG→MAYA: bong
ANGEL→MAYA: The Smiths, The Queen is Dead
LOGAN→MAYA: incense kit
TRISTAN→MAYA: bong
KORI→STELLA: leather one-piece, my blushing face, the gift of vio-
lent gut laughter, the everlasting love of super important people

o   **SUBJECT E ~ "STELLA ULANSKI/BIRTHDAY GIRL
#2":** Like OG, I'd known Stella since middle school. She was
Canadian and had thunder thighs. To quote Tristan: "She
looks like something you'd float at a parade." A couple
years after graduation, I was told she'd had a crush on
me. The timing of this would have been pretty inconve-
nient if there had ever been a chance of me doing anything about it.

Stella tries to fit into her present but her thunder thighs won't be
tamed. Maya tries it on instead. I am horrified. Looking away as she
strips to her underwear, telling her, "I really really think you should
wash that."

Logan punches me in the arm, saying, "I really really think you
should shut the fuck up and not ruin this for us."

The thing goes on, then back in the box, and I know it'll never come
out again. I pretend it'll go and live happily on a ranch somewhere, running and frolicking with Mufasa, Old Yeller, and Bambi's Mom, washed
clean of the **vaginal** fluid and the hardships of this world.

4.   steal a nug off her brother

Maya's brother arrives with disappointment, saying his girlfriend
won't let him sell to kids anymore. Of course, the boys all know they
can convince him to sell. They've just never had to pay before. They
chalk it up to a loss.

Tristan says he'll stay and give the girls a ride. The unconfirmed rumor is: *he's the primary suspect in Maya's fucking around.* Logan would be suspicious, but he doesn't have a label.

o   **SUBJECT F ~ "TRISTAN CARR":** Tristan dropped out of high school like OG 'cause he hated all the English teachers and thought reading was bullshit. He started Job Corps, but quit that too and took up glass blowing instead. By "*took up*," I mean blowing glass in his parent's garage. By "*blowing glass*," I mean making bongs. As far as I know, he still does this.

OG hears some girl named Natalie is coming by. He says he wants to stay with Tristan, but Logan declares "BROS BEFORE HOS" and we pile back into the Prius. This is important. We have to find marijuana.

~ P R E – G A M E ~

5.   *tear shit up*

Frantic calls to all members of "LOCAL STONER SOCIETY," looking for anyone who'll split their stash. With Maya's brother going big time, it's apparently a dry season.

OG gets us started on the bottle of whiskey, the prospect of a sober night drawing over him like an awkward boring cloud, when he swallows and screams for us to **STOP!** He throws open the door and **SPRINTS!** across the street at a chubby black guy, us all sitting **POISED!** and knowing how he always gets a little **RACIST!** by the end of the night, and getting ready to **YANK!** him out before the smiley chains go flying.

No need. He trades the bottle of vodka for a rolled-up sandwich bag and slips back into the car with a long-**dick** swagger.

"Did you know that guy?"

"Yeah. He's in Job Corps."

"Cool. 'Cause otherwise you just saw a black dude and assumed he had weed."

"Yeah, I did that too."

We pack a pipe and sit in the grass behind the football field, Logan pep-talking me through a coughing fit with some choice inspirational words, like, "***pussy***" and "*keep hitting it.*" OG brings up Natalie again, saying how **Little** G's all pumped up, Angel telling him it'll never happen and the two of them throwing down an ounce and a six pack for tonight and whoever gets his tongue down the most throats.

They spit in their palms and shake. I'll never understand this.

We drive to Tube Time, stoned and buzzed. There's a small crowd outside the doors. The place is rented out and closed early for us, but the overnight attendant hasn't come. I take census. The gender ratio is 3:2 of 30 in favor of girls and, consequently, in favor of the bet.

Hunter Jones comes over with his backpack to compare goodies.

OG:
- ½ bottle of whiskey
- bottle of Captain Morgan
- pipe
- g of skunk

HUNTER:
- 10 pack 8g whippit canisters
- bag of microwave popcorn
- half-o of OG Kush (how?)
- 12 pack Durex Rainbow Color Condoms

o **SUBJECT G ~ "HUNTER JONES":** The first time I met Hunter was freshman-year science when he told me how he didn't *really* look like Kurt Cobain. I agreed with him. He showed me his student ID, telling me again, saying he looks nothing like the guy, so I said, okay, maybe you do, and he never brought it up again. He nicknamed me Coral. It stuck for a month. I have nothing bad to say about him.

"Goddamn, Jonesey? Who's the lucky lady?"

OG steals the condom box and I start seeing in my head how it's all gonna play out. Logan will sleep next to Maya, Stella next to River, young boys lined up for a visit to **Cougar Town** with Maya's mom, Angel and OG invading throats, Hunter Jones poised to present **the sword** in five shades of glorious Technicolor, and me. Abandoned. Listening to the crying girl complain. Picking up all the recycles.

OG trades Hunter the bottle of whiskey for 2 condoms and 4 whippits. They are both happy with this.

Logan points at me, saying, "Yo. You got a rubber for Kori? He's losing his virginity tonight."

"K-dawg. That's our boy. Makin' us proud."

Hunter hands over a little square package. I hide it in my pocket before the girls can see.

The first girlfriend I ever had was at my second daycare when I was four and a girl drew me a picture of our wedding in crayons. She was the first and the last when to the utter soul-wrenching desolation of my brittle romantic heart she moved away to California. I have yet to fully recover.

"You know to put it on your **dick**, right?"

"Yeah."

The overnight attendant promptly arrives twenty minutes late. Maya's brother laughs and gives him a man-shake, pointing with his thumb, saying, "I fuckin' sell to this guy."

~ THE THING ITSELF ~

The lights go on and we take off our shoes, running cloud-headed and staggering through this giant play place of ball pits and beehives of plastic tubing, obstacle courses, down slides, up bar climbs, endless.

The intoxicants kick open the cages of our spirit animals released into their sweaty plastic natural habitat. If our littler selves could see us now. We are fiercer than we've ever been. We don't grow up. We improve. We go. Until the drugs wear off. I run and vomit in a stall in the boy's bathroom, look up, see the porcelain speckled with orange pee dots and gag out round two.

My mouth is still sick and burning when the pizza comes. We move to the four-person swivel chair tables and this petri dish of popular kid society gets broken even further into some sort of, like, sociologist's fever dream. Logan sits with Maya, her mom, and her brother. OG and Angel sit with Hunter Jones and the subject herself, Natalie. I stand in the center of everything with my little paper plate of pizza, thinking how in middle school I spent the first two month of recess in the boy's bathroom, sitting in the stall, hiding my feet so no one would notice me and praying to whomever in heaven was listening, for a friend, just one, anybody.

My miracle finally arrives. Tristan's table is empty. I **ACTION DASH!** and **SLAM!** my plate down and **COOL POSE!**, all **NONCHALANT!**, stuffing pizza into my **FUCKING FACE!** before anyone can question or really even **PROCESS!** what I've done.

Tristan laughs, like, "Wow. That's awkward."

I turn. Zoe Delaney, Chloe Burton, and Girl #3 are standing, staring at the three seats that were supposed to be theirs, now two. Zoe does the popularity math. She and Chloe shame Girl #3 with their eyes until she walks away and sits alone somewhere else.

o **SUBJECT H ~ "CHLOE BURTON":** I'd also known Chloe since middle school. Despite the butter-face jokes and the gaps in her teeth 'cause her complete permanent set never grew in, I thought she was pretty [SEE: "*hawt/bangin'/dick-in'able*"]. She once grabbed me laughing and said how she was gonna take me to the girl's bathroom for a prompt fucking. Logan laughed and said look at his face, he's like, who's this bitch? She play-slapped me and called me an asshole. I am never prepared for these moments.

Tristan thinks he has an in with Zoe, so he licks her pizza and laughs as she eats it with her smiling disgusted face. Chloe says eww and turns to me, like, "So cool party, huh?"

"Yeah. It's decent."

Over Chloe's shoulder, OG smiles and fucks the hole of his hand with his finger, Angel next to him, saying, "You look so cool right now, K-dawg. You got this."

"What the hell, Angel? Don't jump on his game."

Chloe leans over and puts her hand on my shoulder, little squeeze, "Leave my buddy Kori alone," me in my head, like, what do I do, what do I do, what do I do, and them pointing and laughing, saying, "Look at his face!"

We go back to the tubes when the pizza's gone, but it's not the same with the highs all faded and the food in our stomachs absorbing the booze. OG's sober cloud is drawing in again, he lets us all know, and he spies on the overnight attendant until he catches the guy smoking a joint in the freezer.

OG negotiates the use of the breezeway for a hot box. They are both happy with this.

The first wave goes in. I look through the window in the door and everything is smoke. Stella grabs me and takes me in with the second wave, saying, "Aw, Kor. You look so lonely without your friends." Someone passes a joint. Everyone else just breathes until they feel it. Chloe takes a hit, then hands the joint to me. My lips stick on the ghost of her lip-gloss. This is closer than a wedding in crayons. Not as close as OG **POWER HUMPING!** up into Natalie and making the stall walls vibrate, but close enough.

~ BEDTIME, CHILDREN ~

The building gets parceled out with all the foam naptime mats, me in the back corner of the kiddie corral and three mats away from Chloe, knowing she will recognize this quiet romantic gesture and finally rid me of my V-card. She goes instantly to sleep.

I stare at the ceiling for an hour. All I can hear is breathing. The drugs are coming out in my sweat now, licking my lips, imagining the taste is still there and it's flavored *cherry*, maybe *strawberry?*, wishing I'd taken my mom's twenty and gone to see a movie or something instead.

"Hey yo, K-dawg? You awake?" OG leans against the corral fence and holds up the half bottle of Captain Morgan. "I can't sleep. You wanna get drunk?"

"I'll certainly give it my best shot."

I sit on the sink, OG on the toilet where he fucked Natalie, maybe others, his child-pee splattered throne. The Captain Morgan is warm and mixed/consolidated with who-knows-what. It tastes like shit on fire.

OG stares at me, serious face, and I almost think he's gonna put another check on his tongue roster when he says, "I don't wanna embarrass you, but you've never had a girlfriend, right? Or boyfriend. Whatever."

"Uh ... no. Not really."

"I'm not trying to embarrass you."

"Yeah. I know."

"I wanna get real with you. 'Cause I've been watching you out there, and you're goin', and all I see is just wasted potential. Take your glasses off." He gets up and takes the bottle away from me, says, "And pull your hair back."

I do.

"Yeah. Yeah, I see it. The girls talk about you, you know. They say you have hot hair. Chloe Burton was just literally telling me in the girl's bathroom how you have hot hair."

I have nothing to say to this, the toilets and the mirrors and his eyes all on me, him saying, "I mean, look at me. I got hot *nuthin'*. I'm ugly as fuck. You can put your glasses back on, by the way. Also, I'm an asshole. I'm a super asshole, but listen. I made out with eight girls tonight. Angel only made out with three. That's not important, but I thought you should know."

"Okay."

"So I'm ugly and I'm an asshole. And you're actually a good guy. And you've got hot hair and a nice face. There's honest to God no fuckin' reason you shouldn't be out there, just killin' it all the time. My suggestion? Get some contacts. And when a girl looks at you, you look right back at her, right in her eyes, and you tell her without a word that you're everything she's ever wanted, you're a god, you got that `dick`, you're a man and you know it. Without a doubt. You believe it, she'll believe it. You feel me?"

"Yeah. I do."

"That's what I'm talkin' about. Bring it in, my homie."

OG hugs me with two claps the way men are supposed to. We are both happy with this. I go back to the kiddie corral, him back into whatever dark mysterious corner or distant universe he came from.

I don't sleep any better.

~THE MORNING AFTER~

I pretend to wake up with everyone else. My mom's still drinking her morning coffee when I call, and she tells me I'll have to wait. I sit at a table. OG and Angel find me on their way out, patented smile/nod, fist bumps, telling me, "You believe it, she'll believe it."

"Yeah. Thanks. I remember."

"Yo, Angel. You think this kid's gonna be hot someday?"

"I don't know. Sure."

They leave, everyone else soon after. I sit on the curb in the parking lot. Logan comes out with Maya and her brother and her mom. He sees me and smiles.

"Who was the lucky girl?"

I show him the condom. "I failed you."

"Son of a bitch." He kicks at the ground like Charlie Brown, *tsk*ing, saying, "Well keep it fuckin' safe. We're not done here."

He gets in the car with Maya's family, and they drive away. The overnight attendant comes out last. He goes to lock the door when someone shouts from inside, "What the fuck? I was peeing."

I turn. It's Chloe. The guy waits for her, then locks the door.

She says to me, "S'up? You getting a ride?"

"Yeah. You?"

"Nah. I'm walking to my mom's work. It's just down the street or whatever."

I say oh, cool, and I'm panicking, finger shakes, looking into her eyes. Like I'm a god. Like I'm a man. Without a doubt. She looks back at me, shaking her head, saying, "Why do you always make that face? God. You're such an asshole."

She laughs and flips me off, walking away, me watching her go and in my head, like **SHIT!**

I am never prepared for these moments.

Counter Culture

Gerard Sarnat

"Theodore Roszak, who saw the youth rebellions
of the late 1960s as a movement worthy of
analysis and its own name, died in Berkeley."
–*Los Angeles Times*, July 14, 2011

Prettiest Ken ever, Oregon high school
wrestler dated Barbie, never drank beer.
But down on Stanford not Maggie's Farm

for higher education, to retain his scholarship,
Kesey became a lab rat: gov'ment
pranksters squirted 500 unspecified

mics into Kenneth's maiden veins.
Observing mosh pit blottoed cuckoos,
the CIA's covert action corps assured

that the DEA declared lysergicmethyl
off-limits for red-blooded Americans
(though trying to inject into green

Cold War Soviet spies to force them say Uncle),
while Stanford's arch-rival in the shapeshift
of Berkeley post-docs in chemistry,

made its better-known, less potent,
easily-patterned cousin LSD on kitchen
counters anyway to mix-up the medicine.

Blackcorn, Storyteller

Graham Guest

I walk across the clearing toward the music. A row of heads and backs appear. I head for an empty bench in the back on the right side. The amphitheater slopes down. Students and instructors and ranch hands are sitting on several rows of semicircular wooden benches watching David Hill. David Hill is sitting in a chair in front of a large, circular, stone fire pit. There's a black curtain or sheet hanging between tree branches to the ground off stage to the right. A fire is burning in the pit and there are different colored lights on in the trees. It is still daylight. Rachel is sitting in the front row on the left side. Floyd and Cosmic and Jolly are sitting in the back row on the left side.

"Chip, Chip, Chip / Braving the wilderness alone. Chip, Chip, Chip / Jesus will carry you home," David Hill sings. He sings "home" for a long time and holds his right arm out over his guitar. The note fades; his head falls onto his chest. Some people clap. "In Jesus' name we pray," he says, unplugs his guitar, stands up, and walks off stage to the left. He puts the guitar in a case and sits in the front row next to Rachel.

The black sheet moves. It moves again. David Hill gets up, walks over and leans into the microphone. "Please welcome, Blackcorn, Storyteller," he says and sits again. Some people clap.

Something flies over the black sheet, lands on the ground and rolls in front of the fire pit. It's hissing; it has a fuse. A second thing flies over the black curtain, lands on the ground, but doesn't roll. It's hissing; it has a fuse too. The second one pops; it's a firecracker. Then the first one, a ball, starts emitting a thick stream of black smoke.

Blackcorn, Storyteller emerges from behind the black sheet. He's a black man. We are the only two black men here. He's wearing a light blue and white-checkered little girl's dress over regular clothes: a dark blue t-shirt, black pants, and work boots. He has on a light blue and white-checkered bonnet and carries a white hooked staff. He meanders around in and out of the smoke, looking at the audience each time he makes a turn. The smoke tapers off. He stops in front of the fire pit. Some of the kids are laughing.

Blackcorn aims his crook at the crowd. "Shut the fuck up!" he says. The kids stop laughing. David Hill stands up. Blackcorn points his crook at David Hill. "Sit down, pussy! This is my show!" David Hill puts his hands on his hips. "Sit down!" Blackcorn says again and David Hill sits down. Blackcorn reaches under his dress and pulls papers out of his back pants pocket. He holds up the papers. "Contract. Signed. Says, 'Blackcorn does and says whatever the hell he wants. Because it's *art*.'" He puts the papers back and turns around. "And get this shit outta here. I don't need this shit." He punches the microphone. It makes a loud thud in the speakers. The microphone and stand fall over and hit the ground. There's another loud thud. A high-pitched tone comes through the speakers. He kicks the folding chair. It flies into the air and hits the ground folded. The high-pitched tone gets louder and louder. I put my hands over my ears. Other people put their hands over their ears and cry out for it to stop. Blackcorn walks behind the fire pit and stops. David Hill and his students get up and clear the chair and the microphone and the microphone stand from the stage. The piercing noise stops. Everybody's talking. Blackcorn walks in front of the fire pit. He holds his arms and his crook up then brings them slowly down. Everyone gets quiet.

"Okay," Blackcorn says and smiles. "Now we got all the housekeeping out the way, we can get down to business. I am, as you know from that very warm and generous introduction, Blackcorn, Storyteller. So. Guess what I'm fixin' to do?"

"Tell a story," someone yells.

"Yeah, that's right." Blackcorn starts walking. "I'm fixin' to tell y'all a little story." He stops. "Anybody want to guess what that story going to be about?"

"Bo Peep, Little Bo Peep," people say.

"That's right. How'd you guess?"

Everyone laughs.

Blackcorn puts his hand to his chin and walks. "Okay, well let's see ... How to begin ..." He stops and holds up a finger. "Hey, I know ... Once upon a time. Yeah, once upon a time," he says and walks. He reaches under his dress into his back pocket and pulls out a flask. He stops, takes a sip, puts it back, and walks.

"Once upon a time, there was a young lady name Bo Peep. She lived on the outskirts of town, in a tiny village, in a tiny house with her momma, Sandra Peep; her daddy, Jimmy Peep; and her little brother, Mo Peep. Everybody in the village was related in some way or another, and they was all of 'em poor. Jimmy Peep worked sixteen hours a day, seven days a week at the Duncan Yo-Yo factory in town, and Sandra Peep worked all day every day cleaning city folks' houses. This meant a lot of times, especially during the summer, Bo had to look after Mo.

"Bo got good at thinking shit up for them to do too: pad-a-cake pad-a-cake, marbles, hide-and-seek, horsey-on-the-leg. Mostly, though,

Mo just liked fucking around with his yo-yo—he took his red Duncan Imperial with him everywhere he went—and he liked running around outside; he especially liked playing down by the creek at the bottom of the hill from Old Mother Hubbard's house. Bo liked going outside too because while Mo was running around and whatnot, she could lie down in the grass and look up at the sky and dream. Momma warned Bo, in regards to these excursions, 'You keep an eye on your brother now. Don't let him out of your sight. And don't wander up the hill too close to Old Mother Hubbard's. I used to clean her house; that lady ain't right.' Bo wasn't worried, though. She figured she knew more about watching over Mo than her momma did at this point in time, and she wasn't about to be scared of some old lady who ain't even come out her own house in the last ten years. Besides, Old Mother Hubbard's was on the other side of the creek, it was too deep to cross on foot, and there was no bridge or log across it anywhere.

Blackcorn reaches into his back pocket and gets his flask. He stops and takes a drink. He puts it back and continues, "So. One day, Bo and Mo go down by the creek. Mo, as usual, commences to mess around the banks; and Bo, as usual, lies down in the grass and looks up at the sky. In a couple minutes, though, something *un*usual happens: Bo's eyes start to get heavy; they start to sag, and before she knows it, she asleep. When she wakes up, Mo is gone.

"Bo calls his name, but there's no answer. She runs down the creek one direction: nothing. Then she runs down the creek the other direction, and much to her consternation, there's a big two-by-four stretching across the creek. She crosses it and runs around on the other side calling Mo's name. But still, no answer. She looks up at Old Mother Hubbard's house, sitting all dark on top of that hill. She's scared now.

"But she calls up the courage—she got to—and she goes up there and rings the old lady's bell. It goes, 'Ding-dong,' and she waits. Nobody comes to the door. She rings it again, 'Ding-dong.' She waits. Nobody. Bo tries one more time and gives up. She cries, "Wah wah wah," all the way home.

"Now, when Bo got home and told her momma and daddy the bad news, they was upset. Her momma fell to her knees and cried, 'I told you, I told you never to take your eyes off a that boy and never get too close to that Old Mother Hubbard's. Oh Lord, Oh Lord. You get him back, Bo. You find a way to get him back or be a curse to this family forever.' Momma was upset. Bo cried too and ran to her daddy for solace. He took Bo in his arms and rocked her like a little baby. 'Shh, shh, little one,' he said. 'It's going to be all right.'

"The first thing daddy did was call the whole village together at the church, and when everybody heard what had happened, they dropped whatever it was they was doing and went out into the hills and fields to look for Mo. They searched high and low until it got dark, but there was no sign of Mo anywhere. When they got back at the church, everybody was saying, 'It had to been Old Mother Hubbard; it had to been Old Mother Hubbard snatched up Mo and locked him inside her house; we got to get up there and break down her door.'

"'Wait a minute, wait a minute,' Reverend Dixon said, trying to act the voice of reason. 'Why in the world would Old Mother Hubbard go and do something like that?'

"Bo's momma stood up with tears all over her puffy red face and cried, 'Because she eats children, Reverend! Don't you know?'

"And the whole congregation ran amok until Bo's daddy stood up and said, 'Hold up! Hold up, goddammit! I got a plan, I got a plan!'

"Everybody calmed down and Jimmy Peep explained that there was this white dude name of Hardiman just started working with him down at the yo-yo factory. He said Hardiman had just got out of jail for being a thief, but that he had not repented the error of his ways therein, and was always bragging about breaking into city folks houses and stealing stuff and about how much he enjoyed doing that. Jimmy Peep said what he was going to do was work a bunch of overtime shifts and pay Hardiman to bust into Old Mother Hubbard's house and either get Mo out of there, or collect some kind of evidence that he can give to the sheriff that Mo is, indeed, stuck up in there. Everybody agreed and Jimmy Peep got to work. In the meantime, Bo's momma suffered visions of Mo's incarceration in Old Mother Hubbard's house, and everybody in the village treated Bo as a pariah.

"Then one morning Bo woke up and came out of her room, and there was a red Duncan Imperial yo-yo lying on the breakfast table. Bo's momma was sitting there crying. 'No sign of Mo,'

"Bo's daddy said, 'but he did find this. I'm heading down to the sheriff's now.'

"Bo cried. Jimmy Peep left and Bo and her momma hugged and cried some more and became very hopeful that the sheriff was going to help them and that pretty soon Mo would be coming home. But when Bo's daddy returned, their hopes were dashed. The sheriff had told him that the yo-yo had been illegally obtained and was thus not admissible as evidence against Mrs. Hubbard, and that even if it had been legally obtained, the yo-yo would not amount to probable cause for a search warrant because it wasn't unique; there was nothing on it to identify it as Mo's. Everybody in town's got a red Duncan Imperial just like that one, the sheriff told Bo's daddy. 'You all have patience. We'll find your Mo,' he said.

"But Jimmy and Sandra Peep didn't have no more patience, and

Graham Guest

when they told everybody else in the village what the sheriff had said, they didn't have no more patience either. In fact, they was all enraged, and it was then and there agreed: that night they would all of them, the whole village, march over to Old Mother Hubbard's, break her door down, kill her, get Mo out of there, and burn the place to the ground.

"And sure enough, once the sun had set, the villagers raised up their torches and, with Little Bo Peep in the lead, marched over to Old Mother Hubbard's. They assembled outside Old Mother Hubbard's, but before they commenced to beat down the door, Reverend Dixon raised his voice and said, 'The path of the righteous man is beset on all sides by the inequities of the selfish and the tyranny of evil men. Blessed is he, who in the name of charity and goodwill, shepherds the weak through the valley of darkness, for he is truly his brother's keeper and the finder of lost children. And I will strike down upon thee with great vengeance and furious anger those who would attempt to poison and destroy my brothers. And you will know my name is the Lord when I lay my vengeance upon thee.'

"The men of the village then carry back the great black pole they had fashioned for the occasion, and the women and children make a path."

Blackcorn, standing behind the fire pit, reaches into the front pocket of his dress and pulls out a handful of something. It falls between his fingers. Dust. He raises it above his head, above the fire, and holds it there.

"The men charge forward with the pole, but Old Mother Hubbard has a charge of her own, and just as they hit the door ..."

Blackcorn throws the dust into the fire, there's a huge explosion of smoke and flame, people scream and fall backwards out of their seats, smoke blows out all over, orange flames rise high out of the fire pit. I stand up, lots of people stand up, confused, watching, waiting until ...

The flames recede.

The smoke clears.

Blackcorn is gone.

The black sheet in the trees is gone.

Everything is quiet.

People start to clap.

Everybody claps and yells.

Someone puts a piece of paper into my hand.

I look around.

The person is gone.

I unfold the paper.

It says, "Meet me under hay bail mountain now – Rachel."

Transformed

Iain Macdonald

The horses flee before the tractor
flail-mowing their overgrown field.
They have encountered this beast before,
as the pasture is close-shorn twice a year,
but still there is no counseling their distress.
Round and round they gallop, all six of them,
resting briefly in a far corner, sides heaving,
before breaking out, heads tossing, hind legs
kicking, as the threat approaches yet again.

They are no longer the placid, near-bovine
animals that graze here every day; instead,
the ground reverberating beneath their
pounding hooves, they have become
creatures made magnificent by fear.

5150

Kelsey Hunkins

"Are you taking any prescription medications?" she asked me.

"No," because in all honesty, it's pretty hard to buy pills to get you through the night without any kind of health insurance. Most days i can scrape up enough change from between the couch cushions to buy some good old-fashioned chamomile tea and some Nyquil to wash it down. Of course, that's over the counter in most places and i only use it about four nights a week. It helps me get a healthy five hours every night and usually knocks me out before the early morning demons come around.

"What about drugs? The dope uh ... marijuana, cocaine, ecstasy ... alcohol?"

"Not really," but not because i don't want to or haven't thought of it. Frankly i just can't work myself up off the couch to pour myself a drink, and after i ruined my intolerance because of the divorce it's just too much work for me to wait for a commercial, to get up, to walk to the kitchen, to decide what i want, to find a clean glass, and then i'll probably have to feed the dog while i'm up because he'll give me the eyes that make me want to kick him and myself, only to come back to an empty living room and watch a reality show about people who just aren't alone enough, and have to repeat these steps about 5 more times to actually get a buzz, only to wake up disappointed in a bath tub full of bloody water.

"Would you consider yourself depressed?"

"i don't think so. Maybe just a little sad," because i looked out the kitchen window yesterday to discover my squash plants were dug out by the dog i got myself for companionship and comfort. i cried near the table he was hiding under for an hour before i went outside and found that my tiny plot also smelled like cat pee, and i don't even own a fuck-ing cat. i decided that the stuff is basically poison, and the squash are dead anyway so there was really no point in going out and watering my garden anymore. At least it's one less thing i had to do in a day.

"Have you done any kind of self-harm?"

"No, not at all." Lately. The last time i did was ... whenever the garden thing happened. At first i was fine, but then a commercial for Miracle-Gro came on and i started to feel incredibly itchy like i wanted to tear my skin off. i held my breath for no reason at all and paced around for a while before looking aimlessly into the fridge only to realize that all i really needed was to slam the door on my head a couple times. Just enough to feel the thoughts escaping my head and that concussion-y blur behind my eyes. It happened again later that night when my dog wouldn't come to bed with me and i only had a half a dose of my medicine left.

"Good. What about suicidal thoughts? Have you wanted to kill yourself?"

"No," i said, and sat on my hands.

Useless Conversation Topics

Elizabeth DeBunce

Strange languages on the paper today. Stared at the calories on the back of my sandwich wrapper, thought of how you love salami with Swiss. Thought of how poetic and full of shit you get around Italian baked bread. Thought of how you loved Sylvia Plath, up till the day you reenacted her last poem in the river behind our house. Thought of how you considered suicide poetry. Thought of how poetry kept you alive until it didn't. Opened our daughter's favorite bedtime story; thought of the hands that threaded the red strings through the wolf's belly. Thought of how I filled you with my bad poetry until you dropped beneath your reflection. Thought of how our son, I hope, is not a reflection of you. Or me. Maybe of the mailman, his shoulder-bag full of love and adulterous letters from and to other people. All lost or late. How language is the medium in which we all drown. How drown is a passive verb. How passively we all live. How you would think that is poetic. How it isn't. Not one bit. How you floated into a river like a slit wrist.

Even When Trapped Behind Clouds

Patty Somlo

Light has a way of finding its reflection, even when trapped behind clouds. That's what I came to understand after a time here. Often, as today, the sun's rays, muted by clouds, shimmer, silvery as the bay. Without wind, everything above the water gets reflected back, including the slender, dark poles of the oyster beds.

I am looking out across a flat calm bay, bordered on the east by dark hills. This is not the first time I have stood here, yet I am nearly moved to tears. I came for this moment—when silver light, the fragile sea grass reflected on glassy water, and, if I am lucky, the arrival of a great blue heron to peck around in the muck, grabs hold of my gut. I depend on these times. They return me to what for lack of a better word I call *home.*

I did not grow up here along Willapa Bay's shores. In fact, my first visit was less than a decade ago.

The bay flows out to the northern tip of a peninsula so slender, the tsunami evacuation signs point both east and west. The land feels isolated and remote, even with a smattering of houses and bleached, weathered cottages. A wildness exists, in part, because of the weather. This Southwestern Washington coast, along with its Northwestern Oregon sister across the Columbia River, is a soaking wet place. Fierce winter storms are legendary, with bucket loads of rain blowing sideways and wind gusts strong enough to knock a man to the ground. Local names give the distinct impression of a melancholy place—Dismal Nitch and Cape Disappointment, being two fine dark examples. William Clark, who camped here in the cold, soggy winter of 1805 with the rest of the Corps of Discovery, dubbed that ordeal the worst winter he'd ever spent.

Weather races across this narrow strip of fir and cedar-shaded land. The sun emerges, and seconds later, a drenching downpour starts.

What struck me the first time I stood on this high bank, admiring the bay that runs the length of the northern Long Beach Peninsula into the Pacific Ocean, was that the water and light, the chartreuse sea grass and mud flats, all seemed so familiar. This was a welcome relief, since I had been scrambling to find something I could love in that first year since my husband Richard and I had reluctantly moved to Oregon from San Francisco.

Economic refugees, I called us, driven out by the exorbitant cost of housing in the Bay Area. It wasn't easy to leave a city I'd fallen in love with the moment I arrived twenty years before, but I was not unaccustomed to leaving. I had grown up a military child.

My migrant childhood fooled me into thinking the move to Oregon would be easy. The last thing I expected was heartache. But that's what I got. For months, I wondered, where was anything remotely like we'd had at home? Would it ever stop raining? And how could we possibly get used to living in such a dreary spot?

We headed out from our inner-city Portland neighborhood to explore the rest of the state, then we ventured to Washington next door. After one long drive, we landed on the Long Beach Peninsula.

Midway across the Astoria-Megler Bridge that spans the Columbia River, our first view of the Peninsula was of hills, blanketed by a forest of dark green trees. At the center point of the span heading north, a sign welcomed us to Washington. The sun sparkled across the river, nearly blinding us. Seagulls glided past the car.

After we drove down off the bridge, we headed north up Highway 101, the river running along on the left side. Everywhere we turned on the slender spit of land, we saw water. All the way up the Peninsula, we passed through tiny towns where Victorian houses, many whose paint had long ago faded and flaked off, lined nearly silent streets.

The second morning, we landed at this spot alongside Willapa Bay. For the first time since leaving California, I found something I could love. The bay reminded me of my favorite Northern California spot— the Point Reyes National Seashore. Standing and gazing at Willapa Bay, I traveled back to hiking alongside Point Reyes' Abbotts Lagoon and experienced a sense of an old, familiar awe.

This, of course, is not Point Reyes and I am not the same woman who hiked nearly all of that area's wonderful trails. But I have the same aching need to ground myself in familiar soil. Throughout my life, moving from state to state, and even country to country, I created relationships with natural places. Next to water—the ocean especially, but also bays and lagoons, rivers and lakes—I have felt best.

I am not so good with people. As a child, I learned to make friends in split-second time. I had to, or else I would have died. Of loneliness, that is.

Every two years, we moved. There were times we packed up one sad apartment and moved to another one across the country one short year after we arrived. I was always the new kid on the block. I started nearly every school year not knowing a soul.

As easily as I made friends, I lost them. The moment we got close, it was time to say goodbye. We usually wrote letters, on small, folded pastel sheets of stationary. At first, anyway. After a year or so, we stopped and permanently lost touch.

I entered adulthood without a single childhood friend. And then I continued on—moving from place to place, and making and abandoning friends and acquaintances. Even in the same city, I didn't keep friends for long.

As if my lack of close friends wasn't bad enough, until well into my forties, I didn't have an ounce of luck at love. Over and over again, I attached myself to guys who, after a few weeks or months, left me bruised and baffled, and lonelier than before.

Along the way, I recognized that walking on the beach, watching waves curl over and fall, soothed me. Or sitting on the bank of a river, keeping my eyes fixed on a sparkling ripple of whitewater, I grew calm. Parts of me that came unhinged in the city would settle down, into a sweet easy comfort.

When I arrive at a place like Willapa Bay, whatever grief or problem I'm burdened with seems to fall apart. Perhaps this has something to do with infinity. No matter how hard I try, I can't see where water ends. In the city, my daily life often feels boxed in, with no way out of relationships that feel unsatisfying. Alongside water, I imagine that I could sail out forever, eventually pulling up on a palm-covered island, where barriers and limits can't survive.

In my early forties, I received a diagnosis of depression. The capital D kind. Until my therapist gave me my diagnosis, I had assumed the melancholy I'd experienced as far back as junior high was temporary. Instead of pinning my low moods and dissatisfaction on my brain, I blamed the outer circumstances of my life. *If I only lived there, if only I had this, if only …* That's how my thinking went.

What led to the diagnosis was that I finally went for help. I felt I had no choice. The end of another relationship had shoved me so far down, I feared ever making it back up.

In therapy, I slowly and carefully began peeling back the layers of emotional scar tissue that had protected me from feeling the pain from years and years of buried grief. Sitting in a straight-back chair across from my therapist Lori, I re-visited my life, tracing back my self-defeating thoughts and habits to a childhood that required a hard stoicism to survive. The tender, bruised parts of my heart bled, over and over again. Each week, I felt a bit lighter.

I began to see myself on a journey toward healing. In this too, I had no choice. Now that the truth had come out, that this change or that change was not going to make me happy, I had to do everything possible to heal.

The worst of the darkness did eventually leave me. I also learned how to live a much more conscious life, in which I welcome feelings, rather than banishing them. I even fell in love with a man not the least bit interested in leaving me, who I married, and whose kind presence reminds me every day of how far I've come.

But there are injuries that never fully heal. For that reason, I need places like Willapa Bay.

Standing here watching a great blue heron glide in and settle herself, tucking her stylish gray-blue wings, I feel the balm of quiet grace. Before long I know the heron will pump her spindly legs and without a single extra movement take flight, helping to heal my battered, aching heart.

Travelling in the Daylight

Charlene Langfur

This is how it is these days, so much letting go, walking
across the morning grass over the back field behind where I
live, past the eclipse of the moon, an April rarity, you can see
it with the naked eye, its touch of orange, then daytime
unfolding like a flower opens, and life starts new. Slowly.
Like that. But it is also quiet, walking past the cholla flowers,
you can see the first of the hummingbirds flitting under orange
blossoms, ready to land. They know what to do. How else
do we go on in the world without guides, signs of resurgence, some
way to save a day or an earth or wait for the return of the moon,
it always makes me want to do more. I am planning
on cooking organic pinto beans today and planting calendula
flowers in some giant old pot, a hint of love, real or not,
I know what emerges will settle, if you take foot to the ground,
the idea of beginning again starts over

Signage

Victoria Waddle

Of course Laura was surprised to see the giraffe rounding the hillside, stopping under a too high eucalyptus and stretching its long curling tongue.

She had laughed at the oil rigs, disguised as little oases, as she pulled off the freeway onto Cabrillo Boulevard. Her hotel was at the far end of the beach, a few miles up the coast. But she'd wanted to travel the oceanfront and see what had changed along this stretch of Santa Barbara. She had been back several times in the twenty-five years since her university days, reuniting with college roommates. They'd all three accumulated weight; Gloria fought rheumatoid arthritis. And so they'd settled into shopping rather than sunning, foregoing the seaweed and the tar that in earlier days stuck to their heels after a stroll in the sand.

Today, she'd come a day early, or half a day, driving in on Thursday afternoon. When arranging the trip, she'd received an email ad offering three nights for the price of two at Las Olas, a little place where she and her roommates periodically reunited. On summer evenings, they'd sit on the patio drinking the complimentary wine and snacking on brie and crackers. At night, they'd have toothache-sweet cookies with milk. The bite of nostalgia on this twenty-fifth anniversary since their graduation pulled them back to reunite in the winter, all three shrugging when they asked, "Why shouldn't we go twice this year?" Since Laura was the only teacher and off for winter break, she was the only one able to make use of the free night. Before her old friends showed, she planned to jog along the three-mile beach path and put her toes in the cold water.

As soon as she could, Laura pulled over and walked back to see the giraffe to assure herself of its existence. It had wandered further up the hill, half hidden in brush. Escape was unlikely. The unseen boundaries of the zoo had broadened.

Laura had been to the Santa Barbara Zoo once with Tom, her boyfriend in high school and early college days. He had come up from USC that weekend to tell her that he was done with Mandy, that he had decided Laura was the one. Her pleasure in being chosen, finally, made her put away her essay, due Monday, and take the first late grade of her life.

It seemed like a normal couple thing to do then, to visit the zoo. Laura, penniless and without a car, had no experience of the city when she'd suggested it. She'd taken a picture of Tom that day, leaning against a faux log-rail fence. Geese waddled behind him in the grass, and he smiled that sideways smirk that made her unsure. Still, she thought of how it would develop, the little pastoral scene, and how she would frame it and send it to his mother as a gift.

That night he'd told her to get on all fours—no, not on the bed, on the floor—and had bitten her back while he bent over her, had pinched her as he pulled away, frustrated and unfinished, raising a purple bruise on her ass.

She wasn't doing things right, this wasn't working, he'd said. She sat on the bed then, a mixture of inexperience and contrition. Tom put a hand over her face, touching with just the fingertips as if palming a basketball. He pushed her back on the bed, and rather than top her, pulled at her ankles so that her knees were at the edge, her feet on the floor.

Then he lay flat on top of her, mounting her face and covering her completely. Laura willed herself still and open, knew she was in a position to hurt him but wanting to pass the test. She tried to breathe in rhythm with Tom's thrusts, but was unable to control her rising panic, her sense of suffocation at each plunge. She pointed her flat hands toward her mouth on either side of her face and then edged them over her cheeks, timing the move inward with Tom's thrusts and withdrawals. The pressure of his hips on her upper arms jerked her bent elbows into the old mattress, and she felt a cramping spasm run across her back at the shoulder blades, but her fingers on her face gave her the pocket of air she needed. Tom reached down and pulled them away. Just as she thought she would have to bite him, realizing he was too heavy to pull off, he finally spent his annoyance, and if still displeased, was at least separated from her and unmoving, allowing Laura to come up from the dizzying hum that clouded her brain.

The unlikely giraffe strolled out of sight, and Laura shook off the memory of that day. It was the ocean and the open stride of her youth that she had come back for, this place she had clung to until the money ran out, and she'd had to go back to the her hometown on the northern edge of Orange County and live with her parents while working on her teaching credential.

As long as she was out of the car and walking, Laura crossed the street to watch the volleyball players. Early January, and still it was a California-dreaming day that brought out the crowds. Every court was in use, everyone young: the girls in crocheted triangles, the guys in baggie boardshorts. Laura leaned on a signpost and looked up. New and glinting in the evening sun was a notice that read, "Tsunami Evacuation Route." It pictured a large wave, a hill, and a man in mid-flight. He looked like a cartoon character who has been walking on air until he realizes that the ground has disappeared from under him. A strange choice, Laura thought, since the object of the sign was to show him making his way to safety on higher ground.

Back in the car, Laura drove slowly in the early darkness. She'd never gotten used to nightfall here. When she was twenty and had ridden her bike from the university to her apartment in Goleta, she'd stop to view the sunset. It should have been straight out over the water, but because the land jutted out at an angle, she'd had to look back toward the university, as if to the north.

Laura turned off on the last possible street before Cabrillo Boulevard disappeared on a twisting hillside and changed its name. A block inland was another sign with the same design as the one she had leaned against, but this one said, "Leaving Tsunami Hazard Zone."

She wondered how they measured such a thing. What constituted the beginning of safety? Water lapping at your feet? Or would you still be neck deep in it, but able to rise above the wave?

Laura made it to the hotel in time for her cheese and crackers. She was alone in the tiny lobby and curled into a prairie chair nestled between the stereo and the fireplace. K-USC was playing, and Laura thought of her resolve to learn more about classical music. She opened a book of Yeats poems, opened another resolve to broaden herself.

A couple in their seventies came over and sat on the sofa. Laura knew them immediately, although she'd been so young the last time they'd seen one another that she'd declined the glass of champagne they offered, telling them about her Catholic Confirmation promise not to drink alcohol until she turned twenty-one.

"Well, we won't tell your parents," the man had winked at her. "So the promise stands." Of course, it wasn't true, but she didn't know how to decline as he was pouring her a glass to toast his wife's father, at whose retirement party Laura was a guest, the plus one. Tom's grandfather must have been long dead by now. But here were his parents.

Ironic, considering and *small world* galloped by, but instead of reintroducing herself, Laura turned back to her book, tightened the cocoon of her body. The night of the retirement party, with its champagne and white tablecloths, Laura had sat at the oblong table closest to that of the honored guests, with Tom on one side and his younger brother on the other. The brother, shaggy haired, silent, and brooding, had pinched Laura. Laura had whispered this to Tom, not knowing what else to do. When Tom's parents came over to congratulate him on the toast he'd made in honor of his grandfather, one that highlighted his own importance as the oldest grandson, he repeated the story to them. They laughed and shook their heads in the boys-will-be-boys meter.

Now, Tom's sister and another woman with a little girl came in, mid-conversation. The brooding brother didn't appear to have made the trip. The sister, Laura was acquainted with. The other woman, she'd never met, but Laura recognized her and knew her name. Clara.

About thirteen years ago, Laura's mother had saved the newspaper society page for her. When Laura came over to drop her kids off before heading to class—she was finally working on her master's degree—her mother pushed the paper in her direction and tapped the picture of Clara. "I guess that could have been you, huh?"

In the photo, Tom had his arm around Clara, easily ten years younger than Laura. Tan and exuding good health even in newsprint, Clara had blonde highlights and an emerald necklace that she might have borrowed from Elizabeth Taylor. The caption stated that the newly wed Mr. and Mrs. Thomas Williams were attending a gala for the Children's Hospital of Orange County.

"No, Mom, it couldn't have been me."

"I'm just teasing you, Laura. But they look like a nice couple."

"I'm sure they are." What else was there to say? Certainly not any larger truth about who Tom was. Maybe one of the minor tales, the story of the time he showed Laura the free CDs he'd gotten from Columbia House by signing his roommate's name to a mail-in offer, which included the requirement of purchasing three more CDs at regular price within a year.

It was a small thing. It was an easy fraud. It was Tom, practicing.

He had to be nearby, somewhere in the hotel.

The girl, Tom's daughter, was whining about feeling sick.

"I told you not to eat the ice cream if you have the flu," her mother said. The girl threw herself on the love seat and kicked. Laura thought she was nine or ten, but her behavior seemed more suited to a five-year-old. Her mother pushed in next to her, and Tom's sister took the last chair.

Laura was surrounded. She put her book on the end table and picked up her ceramic plate of cheese and crackers. Tom had to be here any minute to join his wife and daughter. Laura meant to stand her ground.

"Well, that's the Swiss for you. Everyone knows. It was hell trying to get the house built in Geneva. All the neighbors want a say in everything. We're going to avoid that here."

Laura thought of Julie Andrews in *The Sound of Music*, and how she'd had to stop singing during her escape from the Nazis, quieting children behind gravestones. Were there nosey Swiss folks to greet her when she'd gotten the family down the mountain? The word Swiss only reminded Laura of the dairy trucks on the freeway, delivering milk, their sides painted with a lopsided cradle of a crescent. "Can you say Swiss without smiling?" they asked. Apparently, the Williams family could.

"You know how people are in Montecito," Tom's mother said.

As a college student, Laura hadn't known where Montecito was when she took a class with a visiting professor from Colorado. He used Montecito to mock the area. He'd seen a man there, his Mercedes stopped at a red light, picking his nose, first one nostril and then the other, digging deep. Afraid to display her ignorance in front of the class, Laura went to the library and found an atlas, was surprised that this nucleus of wealth was adjacent to Santa Barbara.

"Everywhere you go, the same. Montecito, Boston, Geneva. This way, we'll be able to get the house done before anyone can complain," Tom's father said.

Her reading interrupted, the music faint under the complaints, Laura felt the white flag of her heart's desire. She'd be better off in the dim light of her room. She stood up.

Tom's mother was unsteady and bumped her shoulder in her hurry to take Laura's seat in the superior light of the lamp. She farted and without apology, sat down.

"Is she poor?" the daughter asked loudly as Laura rounded the corner out of their sight.

"No one here is poor," her mother said. "Stop asking that about everybody. Don't eat my cookie. You'll throw up."

Laura, now passing the front desk, tucked her chin into her chest. Tom was standing by the tray of cheese, picking out slices with his fingers. Though his hair was still a tasty maple brown, it was receding, flecked with gray. His eyes, brown as well, had become lighter over the years, gold flecked. Neither had been his distinguishing trait. Over six feet tall, his good looks came from the drama of his angular features, his cleft chin. His abdomen was still flat and his polo shirt was tucked into his belted pants. He might have just stepped off a poster from a dry cleaners' ad, except for the slice of cheese he held while he stared at Laura.

"What are you doing here?" he demanded as if she had spent the intervening years tailing him.

Laura reached up to touch her ponytail, which she had wound with a rubber band to keep her hair out of her face while she read. "Vaca-

tioning. What are you doing here? Did someone tear down the Bilt-
more?"

"I still know a good deal. Three nights for the price of two, and then
with the miles, it's free. We're just seeing about a house."

"I heard some of that. Don't piss off Oprah."

"What the hell is that supposed to mean?"

"Oprah has that ranch in Montecito. You'll be neighbors."

"We won't be in her line of sight, I think."

"It was nice running into you," Laura said on her way out. She
slowed down in front of the hotel laundry room, its door open to the
driveway, the steam warming the cool of the evening. She listened to
the Spanish speakers and their *tejano* radio, breathed the scent of fabric
softener.

Tom approached. "Hey, wait. Come on, come meet my family." He
grabbed her above the elbow and pulled, and Laura had the old familiar
sensation of his thumb in the underside of her upper arm. Exhaustion
penetrated her. She didn't argue.

After Tom had exclaimed, "You'll never guess who this is," his parents
didn't, but his sister smiled. When he said, "Laura McConnell," the
older couple lit up in recognition, Tom's mother turning to Clara and
saying, "Tom's high school sweetheart." Clara laughed and asked for
a story from the high school or freshman college days, but Laura just
waved her hand.

They were all surprised that they hadn't run into Laura before. "We
come here several times a year," Tom's dad said. "Ever since way back.
When this was the Tropicana, and they had pink tile and flamingos." He
chuckled.

Laura answered their questions. Yes, still married. Yes, she had two
kids. Boys. A college sophomore and a high school junior. Yes, she did
end up teaching elementary school. Second grade this year.

"Tom didn't find the right girl for awhile," his mom said. "So he just
has the one child. Marion Lucy is nine."

Marion Lucy pointed at Laura. "She has copper spots," she whispered to her mother. "And poor people have copper skin." This time,
Laura knew there was something wrong with the child, so she smiled,
but the family had finally come to a loss for words.

"I was just heading off to sleep," Laura said. "Long day and all that."

"Let me walk you to the elevator," Tom said.

Clara looked Laura up and down and then said, "I don't see why
not."

"Marion, sweetie," Laura said, "There's full-copper people right
down the driveway. You can see some when you go to your room."

"That was a weird comment." Tom said as he again took Laura above the elbow and opened the door to the patio. "You're a teacher. Can't you tell she has a disability?"

"Of course, but—really? Copper spots? Haven't you even allowed your kid to be around people with freckles?"

"I think it's just that you don't have any make-up on—you know. But she sees people. Other places. It's an obsessive thing. She saw a documentary on Cesar Chavez in school, and she's still trying to make sense of it. The last seven months, every time she sees someone with 'copper' in their skin, she starts that up. If she sees the gardeners or the house cleaners, she wants to—"

"Pinch them?" Laura asked.

"No." Tom gave the quizzical look and Laura added, "I remember that both you and your brother were pinchers." Tom smiled and pressed the elevator button. "Marion's more of a grasper."

The elevator doors opened. Laura was surprised when he stepped in. At first they were silent, using stranger elevator etiquette. Laura imagined a scene from an old movie, where the man of the house rang a bell for dinner to be served. The maid pushed a cart into the dining room. It took her a second to realize why the image had come, but when she did, it was a private humiliation. Despite Clara's dismissal of her, Tom's stepping into the elevator filled Laura with the heady sense that he would proposition her. That she would have the chance to turn him down. But she had mistaken the ringing of the bell, thought of it as a desire for the maid and not the dinner, the thing delivered. No. She knew what he wanted.

At the hotel room door, Tom said, "You know, I always thought you'd call or write me after that last disaster of a date. It didn't seem like you were ready to give up so soon."

Laura had meant to say she'd come to her senses, but said instead, "This stuff about how it took you a long time to find the right woman doesn't fool me. I know you married Mandy. And I know you killed her, too."

Laura had sensed correctly. This was the question he really wanted answered, why he'd walked with her.

Tom put a hand in the doorjamb and leaned on his arm. "Mandy was a victim of an accident," he said quietly.

"I don't suppose we'll have a chance to exchange philosophies about perception and reality. Goodbye, Tom." Laura stepped through the door and closed it carefully, allowing Tom time to move his fingers.

The last time she had seen him was the same day of the zoo. It was hard not to alter the story now, to make herself less pathetic, even after all these years. It played back from a wide-angle camera, a view from the ceiling that she'd seen in televised police interrogations, a view that she couldn't really have had when Tom had dismounted her and gone to the kitchen, coming back with a glass of ice. Laura had pulled the sheet over herself, but Tom lifted it away and stared. He took a piece of ice and pressed it against her clitoris.

When Laura hiccupped and cried, he took it away, saying he'd seen that in a movie. Laura pulled the sheet over herself again. This time when Tom pulled it away, he saw that she had pressed two fingers to her clitoris.

"You're gross," he said.

Naked, she'd begged and wiped snot on her forearm as he put on his clothes and readied to leave. When he backed away from her, she'd fallen to her knees, followed him like a medieval penitent, like a peasant on the last bloodied mile of her pilgrimage to the basilica of the Virgin Mary in Mexico City.

"Please. I'm sorry. I won't do it again. Please."

All this, too, she now pictured from a ceiling view, focusing on her hair, the place where the roots parted and she could see the white scalp.

When he'd left, he put his foot out, not to kick her, but to give himself room to exit without Laura blocking the door.

And then there were all those letters, one upon another she wrote, forever editing, never sending, hoping always in the most recent version to get it right. Why, after all, had she touched herself? It wasn't for pleasure, but to use her fingers as a compress, staunching the emotional hemorrhage of the day. Couldn't he see? It wasn't about satisfying herself, she only wanted to satisfy him, that was her pleasure, her touch just a preconscious action.

Meeting him had been like reading *Jabberwocky* for the first time. She could almost make sense of him, he seemed like something she knew, and would know, or believed she would know on the next date, and then the next, one after the other, stacking them up. She wanted to understand. She was trying.

The more she wrote, the clearer it was to her that the letters wouldn't work. He was with Mandy now. Hadn't he told her months before that even if Laura was pretty, she was an eight on the scale of ten? But Mandy was a nine. Tom must have argued with Mandy the day he'd come to see Laura. He hadn't meant to stay with her, but rather to make Mandy jealous.

How slowly Laura had learned that her life was not a rind to be flung on the compost heap that fed him. Was it five years that she had mourned?

Laura sat at the little Queen Anne table in front of the window, looking out over the well-lit parking lot. She took out her iPad and connected to the hotel's wifi, tried to transition to the here and now. But what was she going to do? Post on Facebook? "Guess who I just ran into?!! ROTFLMAO!" There was a small fountain at the front on the hotel, two frolicking dolphins, spewing streams of water. Laura opened the window, but was too far away to hear the spray.

If there's a butterfly in the bottom of every Pandora's box, then this was hers: Tom didn't know. Not about any of her pleading midnight revisions, the leap from her bed when at three o'clock in the morning she'd cross out a single word of a draft letter to replace it with one more precise. (Nor the stifled tears, the cold bathroom tile where she'd lie between bouts of vomiting. Quiet, quiet that suppressed heaving. She had sleeping housemates.)

Laura never would have met Tom except that they'd both attended the same dance at her Catholic girls' high school. She thought he must have gone to Damien, the boys' counterpart, but he was just crashing the party with a few friends.

And while most women never had to think about their first boy-friends again, Tom kept popping up in the newspaper because he had made it, was far richer than even his parents. A few years after he was in the society page, the *Orange County Register* ran another article on Tom, in the business section. Laura had come to her parents' for a visit. While her boys and her husband played in the pool, and Laura waited for her sunscreen to dry completely, her father pushed the article across the kitchen table at her. "Your mom saved this for you," he said. "She thinks he's your high school sweetheart."

Laura read. This time there wasn't a picture, but Tom's hedge fund management firm appeared to be involved in insider trading.

"He is under investigation, true, but nothing will come of it," her dad said. "It doesn't look like they have enough—on him, anyway—to make it stick. He makes five point six million dollars a year, says here."

"What can anyone do that makes them worth that kind of money?" Laura wondered.

"Oh, that's just his base salary," her dad said.

How had her mom missed the very first article, then, before the many others she would save? She'd always practiced the sort of flaccid mothering that leaks through boundaries and whose style can't be pinpointed. Careful with some details, but an often-tired person, the stair steps of her six children too close together. And still.

She had to have read the headline "Woman Asphyxiated in Sex

Game." And, of course, she would have read the article, the lurid particulars.

Laura having read the article was more accidental as she hadn't lived in Orange County since she'd come home from college. Yet Gloria, who didn't know Tom very well, but had an amazing ability to catalog details, mailed the article with a Post-It note: "Your old beau?"

Laura's mother hadn't known Mandy. But she must have read that Thomas Williams had strangled his wife, Mandy Gregor Williams, with a necktie during sex play. They were doing what Laura had not heard of back then, cutting off oxygen to produce a more thrilling orgasm. Tom had not pulled loose the noose in time, and Mandy passed into unconsciousness.

Laura knew that the only reason this article had slipped past her mother's watchful regret was that she couldn't imagine anyone so close to them doing such a thing. Thomas Williams was a common enough name. There were the years when Laura, too, had allowed that the devil in Tom was no more than fumbling inexperience like her own, rather than a flawed character.

But after this article arrived in the mail, Laura made her first Internet search at her local library, the Unix-based database delivering the glowering green type of a follow-up article. No charges would be pressed, as the sexual activity was consensual. The woman's grieving parents didn't understand this. "Why didn't he call an ambulance when he saw she was unconscious?" the mother had asked.

That question was answered, too, in a final paragraph of two lines. "When asked why he hadn't tried to call 911 sooner, Williams said that he was too traumatized. 'She looked shocking,' he commented."

She looked gross, Laura thought.

Shame kept Laura from confronting her mother with the truth about Tom. And her mother kept sliding those news articles across the table in every season, consistent evidence of her missed opportunity, mother of the wife of a multimillionaire.

But, of course, Laura couldn't have been Clara. She had been as naïve as her parents prayed she would be, evidence of the miracle of Novenas to the Blessed Mother. Laura had been mapping the world alone when Tom pulled her from the balloon-strewn gymnasium and into his car, had only gotten far enough to view action as a metaphor for love, and not as imminent danger. Her world had only prepared her to be like Mandy, the first wife, the one who consents to the noose. Why hadn't Tom chosen Laura to perfect the control he would wield, to make her a mottled purple death mask of burst capillaries? Perhaps because Laura was the eight, Mandy the nine.

Victoria Waddle

Security lamps in the parking lot splashed on. Tom headed the single file of his family. Marion Lucy was in the middle, her mother behind her, pulling a suitcase. Their single shadow looked like the silhouette of a double-humped camel. "I want to talk to the copper people," Marion howled, anguished at the injustice of her circumscribed world. Suddenly, she stopped, curling her back and opening her mouth in a way that Laura recognized from her years of teaching small children, but it was an act. Still, she had to hand it to Clara for so swiftly jumping away from what would have been the trajectory of Marion's vomit if the threat were real.

Meeting Tom was as destined as it was unfortunate, the sort of surprise that punctuates the life of an eight out of ten. Laura hoped not to have to see him again. Yet always looming was a future of those peculiar moments when her mother would slide news articles across the table to her. And there was the rest of the weekend to contend with.

Now, in the darkness, with the moon pulling the expanse of the Pacific Ocean, wave after wave, to crash within a block of her balcony, Laura considered tomorrow's gift of springtime weather in early winter, and the arrival of her good, true friends.

Acorns

Melissa Hedges

He called me "goddess" once he was done
chasing me across the sea.
There are rumors that I had no childhood,
that I simply waltzed into being
from sea foam and scallop shells.

Hera catches me wrapped in goose feathers,
turning his wedding band over and over.
I wonder if this will be the lightning
bolt that will strike me down.

She calls me a whore and hopes to God
the demon swelling in my womb
is everything I wanted.
"Don't worry," I pat my belly.
"It's full of cobwebs and air."

I toss the wedding band
between the sheets. Out the front door.
One step after another.
I have been cursed by a plethora
of jealous wives. I rub my stomach. Barren.
Sometimes, I think about the acorns that fall
between cracks and won't
get to grow into trees.

Inheriting Wilderness

Kelsey Lahr

A merican wilderness is designed to be useless. Defined in 1964 by the Wilderness Act, wilderness exists to "assure that an increasing population, accompanied by expanding settlement and growing mechanization, does not occupy and modify all areas within the United States and its possessions, leaving no lands designated for preservation and protection in their natural condition ..." In other words, its purpose is to be not-civilized. Furthermore, it is to be "an area where the earth and its community of life are untrammeled by man, where man himself is a visitor who does not remain," where previous human impact is minimal, and which affords "outstanding opportunities for solitude." Tall order.

The United States has over 100 million acres of legally designated wilderness; about 700,000 of these are in Yosemite National Park, where I live. Most of Yosemite, in fact, is wilderness—over 95 percent. The great majority of visitors only see the five percent of the park that is easy to get to, and therefore is not wilderness by definition. A map of Yosemite's wilderness shows a large and almost unbroken hunk of undeveloped territory. But on a map of the United States, wilderness areas look like bits of confetti sprinkled sparsely over the country, with little mounds here and there in the west and north. Only about five percent of America is wilderness, and over half of it is concentrated in Alaska.

Neither wilderness nor the policy that created it cares whether we Americans ever visit this pristine birthright. Mercifully, wilderness must meet no visitation quotas in order to stay protected—quite the opposite. Annie Dillard wrote that humans must bear witness to the natural world in order to give it meaning. "The show would play to an empty house, as do all those falling stars which fall in the daytime." I should think the wilderness would prefer the empty house. It is one of the few places we can turn to in this godforsaken civilization to be reminded for once that everything is not all about us.

I was a few months shy of eighteen when I stayed overnight in Yosemite's wilderness for the first time. My family camped all the time when I was a kid, but always in one of those overcrowded developments with roads running through them and tents piled up on one another like playing cards in a deck. I loved it just the same. But when I was seventeen we went *out* into the wilderness.

I was on a church youth group excursion to Yosemite, which was a first for us, mostly because our church had so few youths to speak of. Pine Grove Baptist Church had an ancient but very kind congregation, and its stranglehold on tradition made it a hard sell to teenagers. But as a last-ditch concession to the twenty-first century, they'd finally hired a youth pastor earlier that year, and Pastor Tim wasted no time planning an outdoor adventure for the few loyal high schoolers that there were.

The backpacking trip was scheduled for the final week of July, and it sat highlighted in neon green on my calendar, the last carefree event of the summer before I would have to turn my attention to packing for college. Pastor Tim had been planning for months. He was a Midwesterner and naturally knew nothing about navigating the Sierra Nevada, so he enlisted my father, with his years of experience backpacking in Yosemite, to guide our inaugural trek. The group had dwindled by the time the departure date rolled around, due to family vacations and other unforeseeables of summer break, leaving five teenagers, Pastor Tim and his wife Rachel, and my father.

And now here we were—we'd climbed the mountain with everything on our backs that we'd need for the next four days, set up our camp, explored the surrounding woods, scouted for the most private places to use as an outhouse, almost froze swimming in the nearby lake, taken pictures, and generally horsed around. And when the evening got thick with mosquitoes we took refuge in the boys' tent, which was the biggest, and played rummy.

Aside from a short climb of a nearby peak, we spent our wilderness excursion lounging. We lounged on huge boulders and by the lake. We lounged around camp and on a granite outcropping at sunset. The whole experience was completely unproductive and completely lacking in solitude. It was glorious.

After dinner on our last night, we sat on logs around a modest campfire and admired the sunset through the spindly silhouettes of the trees, black spires painted over a blushed pink sky. Pastor Tim gently broke into the comfortable silence with the words of a Psalm, which he read by flashlight from the battered Bible laying open on his lap. "The heavens declare the glory of God, and the firmament shows His handiwork. Day unto day utters speech, and night unto night reveals knowledge. There is no speech nor language where their voice is not heard. Their sound has gone out through all the earth, and their words to the end of the world." He trailed off, a further homily supremely unnecessary.

The fire died and we began to get drowsy, and gradually people

Kelsey Lahr

started shifting where they sat, preparing to get up and head for their tents once they found the energy to stand. Just before we dispersed my friend, Shelden, paused and looked around the circle and said, "I want to see the stars tonight, really late. Who's in?" The four others nodded, accepting the invitation, and looked to the adults for permission we knew we didn't really need. Pastor Tim shrugged, and my father asked respectfully, "Can I come?" We all nodded. "I'll get everyone in the middle of the night," Shelden told us.

Well past midnight I woke to the violent shaking of the tent and the snickers of Shelden and T.J. and my father, who stood outside jiggling the frame. "We're up—you can stop," I groaned as the other girls sat up and rubbed their eyes. The shaking and the snickering, of course, intensified.

Our flashlights cut circles into the darkness as we stumbled away from our tents. We scrambled over boulders, holding our flashlights in our teeth, until we found a flat granite slab big enough for us all. We lay close and stared up at the night sky spread above us, the Milky Way running from horizon to horizon like a loose ribbon. I could pick out constellations whose names I didn't know, and I was sure my father would be able to tell us what they were, but it wouldn't have been worth it to break the silence that sealed us in so perfectly and made us almost believe that we could lie there, shoulder to shoulder, forever.

I suspect that most wilderness enthusiasts have introductory experiences like mine. With families or Scout troops, they march into the wilderness in herds and do things there—campfires, rummy—for which wilderness is only a semi-necessary backdrop. And this is fine. There were no motivational requirements written into the Wilderness Act. If church kids go backpacking in order to see God's creation and Scouts go backpacking to learn self-reliance, more power to 'em. But if those kids have even one eye half open, they will see something in the wilderness that they could not have seen elsewhere—the stars undimmed by city lights, a mountaintop with nobody else on it except a handful of their friends, a certain unfamiliar bird. That's what hooks us wilderness types, I think: the idea that all this was here, the whole time! Trees falling cacophonously in the forest with not a soul there to hear them, and fiery sunsets and emerald rivers. It all *exists*, out there, for no more or less than its own sake.

This comforts me to no end. It takes the sting out of mortality a bit. Here is wilderness, I think to myself. It has been here, just like this, probably since the end of the last ice age. It will stay here, just like this (thanks be to the Wilderness Act), forever. Is it really so tragic that my little life will pass, when all this beautiful rugged country will endure?

This is not true. Not even wilderness can take the sting out of mortality—it is all mortal.

In recent years certain scientists and writers have made the argument that neither wilderness, nor indeed nature, exist at all anymore. We humans have so altered the fabric of the planet that there is no longer any such thing as a wholly natural system, unaffected by us. We have planted and paved and built upon huge swathes of the earth, making life enormously more difficult for more species than we will ever know. The farthest flung of wilderness peaks is receiving more or less precipitation because of human-driven climate change, which alters the variety of plants that can grow on it, which in turn will dictate which creatures can survive there. We have our fingers in every pie. This is true of the deepest Amazonian rainforest and the darkest ocean depth—our footsteps are felt even in places far too remote for us to literally walk.

It is for this reason that scientists have proposed a new epoch: the Anthropocene, the age of humans. This epoch will follow the Holocene, the era of relatively stable and benign climate conditions that saw the rise of human civilization. Apparently these things are decided by geologists who form working groups to debate and publish papers about the merits of such proposals. One working group has suggested that the Anthropocene be given a specific start date—the only geologic epoch to have such a well-defined beginning: July 16, 1945, the first detonation of a nuclear weapon.

This is a blow to the type of rugged individualist American thinking that says, like Edward Abbey, "We need wilderness whether or not we ever set foot in it. We need a refuge even though we may never need to set foot in it. We need the possibility of escape as surely as we need hope; without it the life of the cities would drive all men into crime or drugs or psychoanalysis." Now there is nowhere to go to escape from ourselves.

Mercifully, it is easy enough to forget this doom and gloom upon entering the actual wilderness. The Anthropocene does not unfold on the scale of individual attention—I cannot see precipitation trends changing in front of me. When I venture into the wilderness it is not hard to find a spot without a single other human being anywhere around, a place that is, as the Wilderness Act says, "untrammeled by man," at least on the surface.

Lots of my acquaintances are accomplished backcountry travelers. They go into the wilderness for the challenge, for the stories, some of them for a paycheck. I know a woman who has hiked from Canada to Mexico for fun twice, on two different trails, and never even brags about it. For years my father led groups of inexperienced senior citizens on weeklong backpacking trips through Yosemite's wilderness, and not a single one of them ever died along the way. One summer when I was in college I dated a man whose job was backcountry trail maintenance and who hiked hundreds of miles that season with a hundred pounds of tools on his back. These people have my undying admiration, but I want none of it.

I do not go into the wilderness for a challenge, or for anything really, except the view and the quiet. It doesn't matter if I hike a lot of miles to get there, as long as the spot affords those things. My preferred backcountry activity is lounging. Sometimes I lounge and sketch. This proclivity is the primary lesson I picked up on that church youth group backpacking trip: the wilderness is the best place for doing nothing.

Loafing in the wilderness, by a musical stream, for example, or overlooking an array of peaks, it is scandalously easy to feel insignificant. The setting demands that one take the long view. And the long view is this: we humans have been kicking around the planet for less than one percent of one percent of its existence. There have been a great number of epochs before the Anthropocene, and it holds that there will be a great many after. Perhaps it will take a very long time once we pass from the scene, but eventually the earth will find its human-free rhythm again. It is possible, if unlikely, that this is what the Apostle Paul meant when he wrote that "the whole creation groaneth and travaileth in pain," but at long last "shall be delivered from the bondage of corruption." It does not comfort me to know that creation can only hope for redemption right along with the rest of us.

But no matter how long it may take for things to right themselves, or be set right by God, there is some comfort in knowing that we and our Anthropocene are fleeting, and the rest of the show is not. Look out over the wilderness from a backcountry peak—I dare you—and try to feel significant. These are times when I thank God that my little urgencies and heartbreaks and quests for meaning are so laughably insignificant in the face of glacial ice and the cataclysms of the earth and the unfathomable depths of time. *This too shall pass*: was there ever a truer understatement?

So I go for an overnight jaunt in the wilderness a couple of times each summer. Usually I pick a trail that will take most of the day, and will put me near a body of water with a view by evening. Then I put my pack on my back and amble on my way. When I get to the lake or river of my destination, I set up my tent and then go about lounging by the water, or sometimes in the water if it's warm enough. Around dusk I pull out my camera or my art supplies and do what I can to capture the sunset, reveling by now in my human insignificance. Afterward I make dinner and go to bed by nightfall. In the morning I make coffee and instant oatmeal that is invariably too sweet, and then I do a little more sketching. Before it gets too hot I pack up my camp, and then make my way down the trail again in order to be back at work the next day. That is my simple and un-ambitious method of wilderness recreation.

I learned this approach from my father. He has long been my wilderness companion, and taught me most of what I know about back-country navigation and enjoyment. In my first few summers working in Yosemite he was in charge of picking our route, planning our meals, and generally acting as the responsible party. Back then he put me to shame, climbing the steepest passes without breaking a sweat while I struggled and gasped up the trail behind him. He always suggested water breaks with great humility, graciously pretending that he was the one who needed a rest.

At some point, though, we found ourselves on equal footing. And then one summer I was unsettled to find myself stopping for water breaks I didn't need.

These days we take it slow. And why not? There's no need to rush in the wilderness. At sunset we sit side-by-side next to our backcountry lake of choice, comparing sketches of the ineffable scene before us that will, Lord willing, far outlast us both.

Elephants at the Orange County Fair

Terry Spohn

We've forgotten Mom on her birthday,
poised on her floral couch
beside Grandpa's frail pipe stand.
She waits for the phone call

while our daughters sit impassively
in July's shameless stare, legs splayed
astride the napes of the elephants
at the Orange County Fair.

These baggy hulks tiptoe in silence
whose ancestors, painted in gaudy wedding colors,
routed Alexander's cavalry
along the banks of the Hydaspes River.

The ghosts of blind men finger the matriarch:
Rope, mortar, wall, winnowing basket?
None of us can touch the nature of this soul
that doesn't know what it's like to be invisible,
any more than the blind know what it's like to be seen.

A tiara of dusty flowers sits across her wide, lobed brow.
More blood flows through her body
than through our entire living family.
Somewhere the bones of her ancestors languish alone.

She curtseys while our daughters fidget
beside her bent knee. They squint into cameras
we fight to hold steady until her great domed shadow
has come down over us.

Crows hop in the hot wind like black leaves.
Leggy hounds sprawl near the tent and dream of one another.
Already I've forgotten the gin-faced gypsy palm reader
who thumbed my lifeline and moaned.

Half Shell

Maureen O'Leary

Tom and his brother's wife, Sylvie, made spaghetti for the group's dinner at the splintered picnic table in the waning evening light. Sylvie sipped red wine and stirred the sauce at the propane stove. She knew the advantages of anchovy paste over plain salt. She knew all the tricks.

Tom's brother, Will, sat in a camp chair and poked the fire with a stick. He harassed the logs until they collapsed. Tom's wife, Janet, read a book in their tent.

A transparent but formidable force field rendered Tom and Sylvie invisible to each other as man and woman. At least, it should have. But after bedtime, Sylvie found Tom on his way from the bathroom. She emerged through the trees as a tall white wraith with her long hair and bare arms. He tried not to be spellbound as she approached.

"Come here." She clutched his hips. "You are unbelievable," she said. "I could make you the beloved for a change."

Tom turned heel and ran as if from the supernatural to the tent where Janet lay sleeping. He turned his back on his wife, nursing a hard-on that dismayed him. When he fell asleep, he dreamed of Sylvie. In his dream, she said over and over again, *I could make you the beloved*.

In the morning, Tom ate lukewarm instant oatmeal and drank tin-tasting coffee in a metal cup. Janet sat beside him in her typical morning silence. After coffee, the four moved to Will's van for a trip to the beach. Tom wanted to snuggle with Janet but she straight-armed him across the back seat.

"I need space," she said.

She allowed him to hold her hand. On the way, Will detailed the features of his new van as he drove. It had an excellent stereo and a DVD player in the back for when they had children. It had the best navigation system ever. The best four wheel drive.

Sylvie sat beside Will in front, cupping her chin in her palm, and looking out the window. Her fingers looked like creeping anemones up the side of her face. Tom shuddered. The parking lot at the fog-shrouded shoreline was empty. Tom opened the door on his side before the engine cut out. He sucked cool air in to his lungs.

The four walked. Janet and Tom did not touch. Sylvie and Will held hands in the lead. Sylvie pulled free to look at where the tide met the sand. Will kept his pace toward the big rocks. There were tide pools there. He said they were the best tide pools ever.

Tom watched Sylvie look for deposits from the sea. She knelt to dig for one that peeked from the sand. She pulled out a pink half shell with a jagged edge. Rough wave action had shattered its smooth domed pattern. Sylvie dropped the broken thing to the ground and ran to catch up with her husband.

Tom tried not to watch his brother's wife. Thinking of the night before spoiled the day and he wanted to love the day. He loved the ocean's salty breeze and the rich living and dying thing smell. It made him think of trips they took when he and Will were boys. They used to lift the shiny bulbous bull kelp ropes where they lay coiled under heaps of flies. They cracked them at each other's legs like whips.

Sylvie's rough voice blew on the wind. Will reached out a lazy hand and squeezed her rear end. If Tom tried that in public, Janet would slap him.

Janet's inky hair blew in untucked wisps from under an orange bandana. He loved the way she looked when camping. He loved her faint and secret unwashed smell. Her cheeks were flushed from the fresh air and exercise. She could be a Klamath Indian woman scoping the beach for shellfish. She could be a Viking lady sewing him sails. She could be a lifeguard, keeping everyone safe.

Tom ached for his wife. He leaned into her side and they pressed against each other like a human lean-to until she ducked away.

Janet stooped to gather a handful of stones. She chucked them one-by-one into the sea, her arm as strong as a man's.

"Do you like her?" he asked. "Will's new bride."

"She's okay. Gorgeous, of course. It's disconcerting."

"She's got nothing on you."

"Stop." She threw another stone. "We talked last night while you guys got firewood."

"What about?" He could barely see Will and Sylvie through the mist.

"Did you know she was a model? She was thirteen, snorting all this coke in Paris."

He wanted to tell her about Sylvie's pass in the woods. The secret rested heavy on his tongue.

"The conversation got weird," Janet said. "She said in every marriage, someone is beloved, the other is the lover."

"Did she talk about us? Who was the beloved between you and me?"

Tom asked.

"Really?" Janet said. "You're really asking that? You're worse than a woman."

Lover. Beloved. He couldn't stop thinking about it. "She's not exactly who I'd picture with my brother," he said.

"They are beauty and the beast. A princess and a frog," she said.

Tom took Janet's face in his hands and kissed her hard. She kissed him back. Then she ran from him to the tide pools, forcing him to chase her.

At the end of the beach, Sylvie had climbed a rock table. She stood six feet above them, her long blonde hair blowing like a pennant.

"Christ," Janet said under her breath.

"Come on up, guys," Will said from beside his wife. "You can see everything over here."

Tom felt stupidly eager to follow his brother to the tide pools. He liked watching the quiet clinging creatures and the busy, frantic loose ones. His high school biology students laughed at him in class. His enthusiasm cracked their dopey nonchalance. He insisted that they look through the microscopes at the worlds inside drops of pond water. He wished he could take his groups on field trips to the beach. He wished that he could make them see that life could hold their interest. Or if it did not, then at least make them understand that the natural world went on, regardless of whether or not they cared.

With a surge of exhilaration, Tom pulled himself up handhold by foothold. He could pretend that the pass that Sylvie made in the woods never happened. At the least, he could tell himself she drank too much and didn't even remember it herself. On that day, he was simply exploring a wild beach with his brother and their wives. He was enjoying an innocent outing among good people. He could tell himself this story and believe it.

They climbed onto the rocky outcropping of the bluff. It was a corrugated expanse of crevasses and ankle-breaking grooves in the wave resistant bedrock. Janet squatted at a pool so still it reflected the iron sky. Tom picked his way over feeling like a big dark bear beside his compact wife. Their reflections stared back at them over a pool teeming with purple urchins, their spikes stiff and wafting for food.

Sylvie wandered beyond them to the edge where the waves exploded against the promontory. Tom watched her again and thought he would never let Janet get so close to the edge. A rogue wave could snatch her and slam her against the rocks.

Tom tapped Janet's shoulder. Janet followed Tom's gaze. She called for Will, who stood at another pool with his camera in front of his face.

"Sylvie's pretty far out there," she said. Will looked up and slipped.

He flailed his arms before Tom grabbed and steadied him.

"Sylvie!" Will yelled. But Sylvie did not appear to hear.

Tom and Will started out for Sylvie together. Sylvie was oblivious to the commotion she was causing. She bent to dip her hand in a pool near the ledge and drew out a crescent-shape thing. She caressed it with her fingertips. The ocean roiled behind her.

"God," Will said. "She's an idiot."

"I don't think she realizes," Tom said.

"She never realizes." He stepped over a crevasse to reach Sylvie. He tugged her arm in a way that Tom thought was rough. Sylvie cursed and then shoved her find in Will's face.

It was a lower jawbone, worn smooth as driftwood. It sported just two stalwart molars capped with gold.

"I found it in that pool over there." She pointed like a child.

"You were way too close to the water," Will said.

"You were worried about me?" Sylvie smiled and tilted her head.

Will yanked the jawbone from her shaking hand. "Was there anything else by this? Any other bones?" he asked. She answered no. Just starfish, urchins, tiny crabs. Will held the bone to his nose and sniffed.

Tom tottered back to where Janet waited at pools much further from the waves.

"What did she find?" she asked.

"A human jawbone."

"Human? How can you tell?" She didn't believe him. "It's probably a seal's."

"Well, it has gold teeth," he said.

Will walked away from Sylvie and she covered her face with her hands like a caricature of a sad woman.

"Drama," Janet said.

Will held his arms tightrope-walker straight over the slippery terrain. The white bone stuck out of his hand like a new toy.

"We need to get this to the police right away," he said.

"I think Sylvie needs you," Janet said, her eyes hard.

"Sylvie needs a kick in the butt," he said. "She's mad at me because I said I didn't care if she fell in the ocean. She'll be along in a minute, watch." Will smirked at Tom as if to say *oh these women* while indeed a sullen Sylvie wiped her eyes with her sleeve and started toward them. They watched her approach, a sodden-haired goddess rising from the sea. She folded her arms to her chest. Her legs in their short shorts were pimpled in the cold.

Will fisted the bone and brushed his knuckles against his wife's chin. "You better watch out," he said. "Troublemakers get a swim with the fishes."

"You're being a dick, Will," Janet said.

Tom's heart galloped. A fight between his wife and brother would be a rickety sail between clashing rocks. But just then an enormous wave exploded against the promontory, washing out where Sylvie had just been standing. The four watched as the foam streamed away. Tom heard the crunching of bones.

Will laughed like a barking dog. He acted as though Janet hadn't spoken. He had a plan for what to do. His directives were shrill above the surf and wind. They would return to the car and drive into town. They would need to drop the jawbone at the police station. They would need to give a statement.

Will charged down the beach with his elbows bent. Tom's annoyance rolled in his throat like a stone. He didn't know what they could do for the owner of the jawbone. Hurrying to the car would not help the man who had been doomed to have part of his skull wash up in a tide pool. Tom brought his hand to his own jaw and fingered it.

Janet walked ahead of Tom with her fists jammed into her sweater pockets. He stopped to look back over the expanse of rocky tide pools, the ledge and the crashing surf. Sylvie had wandered to the ledge again and faced the ocean. She stood in the perilous place where she'd found the bone. She never looked back. She bent her knees and jumped into the foam and violence. The ends of her hair were the last he saw of her.

Tom turned around. He walked with a measured pace until he caught his wife. He felt a remarkable stillness inside. A delayed reaction. A sense of relief.

Will had made it to the parking lot already. He waved his arms at them. He was always such a small and impatient man.

"Where's Sylvie?" Janet asked.

Tom turned around as if he expected his brother's wife to be behind them. Janet pushed past him back to the tide pools and rocks. He followed and helped her search among the boulders.

Janet opened and closed her mouth. She held her hand to her forehead. Will ran to them. He skittered across the rocks. He yelled his wife's name into the sea. He rushed forward on uncertain feet as the waves receded, as close to the edge as Sylvie had been. Janet moved to join him but Tom seized her wrist. "Stay back," he ordered. Her lips formed a thin line. But she obeyed.

Tom set out for his brother, past the oblivious microcosms of ocean life in the tide pools. He didn't slip. He grabbed his brother from behind and encompassed Will's hard, wiry body in his arms. He whispered in his brother's ear. They had to find someone, some kind of rescue. They wouldn't be able to help Sylvie this way.

"What did you see?" Will yelled at Janet. "What did you see? Did she jump? Did she do it on purpose?" Janet shook her head and spoke as fast as a child proclaiming innocence. She hadn't seen anything. She had turned around to say something to Sylvie and she wasn't there. They looked at Tom.

"To be honest with you, I had my mind on Janet," he said. "I didn't want her to get hurt on the way down." Because he looked after his wife.

Tom helped Janet off the rocks and they followed after at slower jogs as Will tore down the beach at full speed, wet sand flying from under his heels. Tom foresaw the next futile hours. If Will's cell phone didn't get reception, he'd drive to the ranger station or the police station. Tom and Janet would stand in the parking lot and they would wait in case Sylvie showed up. He would pretend that was a possibility.

Tom wondered if he would ever tell Janet about Sylvie's pass in the middle of the night. He wondered if he'd say how Sylvie had frightened him. Most likely he would not. Most likely he would not ever say her name out loud again.

Tom looked at his wife as she wept, her hand to her mouth as if to hold her own jaws together. The tide was higher than when they last came through. A shell cracked under his shoe and he ignored it. He was no longer interested in what the sea might offer for a present.

Mourning Hiatus - 5:30 am

Sarah Isto

The chair, the fern, the open closet door
blend in floating gray
remote as news from yesterday:
"Search suspended, no one found."

I will myself slack
beneath the crumpled sheet
barely breathing, hoping to prolong
these vague moments

before stretch wakens muscle into ache,
before memory sharpens news with grief,
before dawn edges past the half-closed blind
to separate chair from fern, and fern from door.

Brotherly Love

Kirby Wright

M y father veered off the H-1 onto Punahou Street in his Olds. It was the first day of 7th grade. He drove through a neighborhood of small tidy homes with mango backyards, duplexes, and beige two-story apartment buildings. Barry, my big brother, chewed gum in the front seat. A pencil was tucked behind his right ear and he reminded me of James Dean in *Rebel Without a Cause*. I shared our father's dark complexion and rugged features while Barry had the blond hair and green eyes of our Irish mother.

I felt trapped in the back seat. I feared driving with Dadio because he'd developed a habit of grinding me whenever he fretted over income taxes or a case. He slipped into a turnout and idled while the radio played "Love Child" by the Supremes. Our new school was halfway between Kahala and the firm; car-pooling wasn't necessary because public buses would return us to the suburbs of Diamond Head. My father switched off the radio. He was trying to grow sideburns like the singer Tom Jones. "Now you boys stick together," he advised. "Punahou's a tough school."

Barry pushed open the passenger door and the hinges creaked. "Tough," he mocked, springing out of his seat like a jack-in-the-box. I got out behind him. I was balancing an armload of textbooks with Pee Chee folders and shut the door. The Olds sped off into traffic.

My brother dropped a book and then hurdled a low-lying chain strung between metal posts. He retrieved it and hustled over a cement path cutting through the lava-walled perimeter of campus. The wall made me feel like we were entering a fortress of higher education, one designed to discourage local kids from trespassing while doling out precious knowledge to the progeny of the privileged. An Asian security guard stood in a sentry-like booth under a shower tree. He pointed directions to a *haole* mother in a station wagon.

My new jeans felt baggy. The jeans weren't new at all—they were Barry's hand-me-downs. I didn't mind. The fabric felt soft against my legs and I liked how they'd faded. I kept my belt cinched tight to keep them from falling. I was proud of my white button-down with the green and white hibiscus, the one I wore religiously on Aloha Fridays back at Star of the Sea Elementary. I had on rubber slippers like my brother.

"Barry!" I called.

He looked back. "What?"

"Slow down."

"Cram it." He picked up his pace to the point his jerking hips resembled a race walker. He had on bellbottoms and a gray Ski Hawaii tee our mother had bought him at Liberty House. He zipped across Palm Drive, an access road lined with date palms. The trees cast prison bar like shadows over Lower Field, where mynahs battled over scraps near a garbage can. Soccer nets were on either side of the field.

Bishop Hall loomed on the hill ahead of me, its stocky white façade lined with rows of tiny windows. It was where I'd taken the entrance exam in a room filled with faces showing everything from hope to fear to a resigned indifference. I'd been eager to please my father yet terrified I would flunk. There were no doors on Bishop Hall's *makai* side and a green umbrella-like roof crowned it. It reminded me of an asylum. I pictured a tyrannical principal ruling over a staff determined to instill fear in the students. All my classes except one would be held within its walls, including Mrs. Creele's morning homeroom.

My brother disappeared into a mob ascending the hill adorned with plumeria and hau trees. One boy lugged a surfboard. Men and women who looked like teachers smoked outside Bishop Hall. Two girls rolled their bikes to a rack beside green double-doors.

Barry and I had compared Class Schedules. We had the same French class with Mrs. Hamster and would cross paths again in Study Hall. I wondered if our classmates would think we were twins. I didn't want to be his twin. I didn't even want to be his brother. It wasn't my fault Barry had been held back for goofing up on the entrance exam. I cursed our father for making him go to Punahou and wrecking what little remained of our brotherhood. Repeating made him feel stupid. Dadio had fanned the flames of sibling rivalry at Star of the Sea by comparing our grades. Barry had defended himself by saying we weren't on the same playing field because he was a year ahead of me. Now that was over. Our father could judge us fairly and I was sure that bothered Barry. He wasn't stupid. He just wasn't book-smart and had an aversion to studying. My brother was great with his hands and he'd single-handedly repaired our mother's vacuum and fixed a short circuit in the garage. But, because our father based value on grades, I knew Barry would be handicapped trying to earn his favor.

Barry challenged me to checkers after a long bus ride back to Kahala, one that stopped for public school kids at Kaimuki High and Kaimuki Intermediate. We'd been forced to transfer to three different buses before reaching Kahala Avenue and walking the last mile home. My brother spread out the board on the lanai and we sat cross-legged facing each other.

"Red or black?" Barry asked me.

"Red."

We weren't alone. Julie, our kid sister, was in her playpen squeezing squeak toys and making her family of dolls talk. Her brown hair was cut short like the actress she was named after—Julie Andrews. She was nearly two but still crawling. "Late bloomer," Dadio had whispered. Her dolls registered emotions when she varied the pitches of their voices. She was putting phrases together and sometimes mumbled what sounded like my name. She wore a Minnie Mouse blouse over pink plastic diaper protectors. My mother was trying to potty train Julie, but with mixed results. The stench of soiled diapers drifted into the hallway and permeated my room. I'd gotten used to the smell, especially since I sometimes changed her diapers after school or on weekends. The playpen on the lanai made it appear my kid sister had been stuck in a cage. But she seemed happy, talking and squeaking away so I resisted springing her. Maybe she felt protected. I knew she'd eventually have to negotiate the battleground our father had created at home.

Barry got "kinged" and attacked my pawns from the rear. I tried protecting them but he kept jumping. I didn't mind losing. I wondered if I was losing on purpose to reestablish a foothold in our damaged brotherhood. There were other things gnawing at him besides school. One was his perceived injustice that our Moloka'i grandmother favored me because I took after our father. There was an ocean of hatred to swim before I reached the shore of friendship my brother so carefully guarded. That feat was nearly impossible because he was always quest-ing for new ways to hate me. One of the only things holding us together was hearing each other scream through the redwood wall dividing our rooms whenever Dadio found us jointly culpable of some nefarious act. We were hardly angels. Anything challenging the smooth running of the household was a cause of action, such as the football shattering the foyer window after a misguided pass, throwing firecrackers over neighboring fences, and experimenting with gunpowder. Barry had hoarded the black powder I salvaged by unraveling unexploded fire-crackers, packing the powder down in a Testors Paint jar, and punching a hole in the jar's metal cap. "The cherry on top," he'd snickered, stick-ing in a fuse. I'd wanted to light the charge in the middle of the road after dinner but Barry insisted we drop it in the water meter box. I'd pried open the meter's round top cover and he stuck in the jar. "Put the cover back!" my brother had ordered, after lighting the fuse. I did. The ensuing explosion fired the cover up into the air like a Frisbee. The steel top plate of the casing snapped like peanut brittle and I felt detonation waves moving through the sidewalk beneath my slippers. The glass lens of the meter disintegrated and the reading gauge spun crazily. Lucky for us, our joint-effort bomb didn't wake Dadio. He was still snoring on the living room couch when we snuck back inside and crept into our rooms. What did wake our father happened weeks later, after he received the bill from the Board Water Supply charging him for a million gallons.

Barry jumped the last of my pawns.

"You should challenge Dadio," I suggested.

"The General won't play me."

"No?"

"He hates losing."

"He might beat you."

"Ya-hoo!" Barry cheered, reaching my last row with another pawn. "King me, Kirbo."

"King yourself."

Barry kinged his piece. "Guess why the General never hits Mom."

"Why?"

"That's what he's got us for."

"Why'd he even want us?"

"No kids mean you're a *mahu*. We're window dressing for his image, not because he really wanted us."

"But he likes having us around."

"To whack us every chance he gets," Barry replied. "King me again."

Besides the double-header beatings, my only other bond with my brother was the shared belief our mother had been hijacked by romance. We both felt she was an innocent who'd been tricked into marriage by a smooth-talker a decade her senior. Barry and I had always vied to be her favorite. I consoled my mother after arguments with Dadio, encouraged her to sing, apologized for crying too loud during strappings, and called her "June Spoon" in a playful way. That was her nickname as a child and I knew using it made her feel young.

My mother was an expert at balancing. She was equipped with a built-in scale, one allowing her to continuously weigh the security my father provided against her dislike for him. She resented him for squashing her dreams. The only time Dadio allowed her to sing in his presence was at the annual Christmas Gala where lawyers and spouses gathered around a white piano in the firm's lobby to sing carols. I felt I'd earned the distinction of favorite by offering my mother a door to my interior world, a realm of futuristic frontiers inspired by *Tom Swift* books and evening sojourns to the solar system through the lens of my refractor telescope. I'd invite her out after dinner and we stood on the backyard lawn sharing a portal to celestial bodies millions of miles away. June Spoon enjoyed looking at the moon, Venus, and the rings of Saturn. "Sometimes I feel like flying to the moon," she'd mutter. Threads of sadness ran through her. I sensed her loneliness because I knew what it meant to feel alone and without someone to believe in you. But there was magic in my mother too in the way she imagined escaping into the light flickering through the refractor. Despite her desire to fly away, the scale inside her always tipped in favor of her singular need for self-preservation. My father was her security blanket. Her sense of right and wrong had been knocked out of kilter by her me-first mentality, one allowing for the sacrifice of her children at the paternal altar of domination and cruelty. Months had passed since my father had caught me anchoring balloons in the street and inviting drivers to run them over, but the memory of my brutal beating kept my fear gauge pinned in the danger zone.

It was dinnertime. June Spoon had prepared pork chops, Minute Rice, and Birds Eye peas. She liked preparing mediocre meals fast and at high temperatures and then keeping dinner warm in the oven and in the pots on the stove in order to share cocktails with Dadio on the lanai. I sat at the dinner table feeling indifferent. The smell of burnt rice and overcooked chops was unappetizing. But I feared the third degree, one that would begin with Dadio's accusation I had no appetite because I'd "filled up on crap" before the meal. I cut off a hunk of bone-dry pork. My father sat across from me scooping up peas with a spoon. I disliked my place at the table because I was in his direct line of fire. Barry and my mother were on the neighboring corners. Julie sat perched in her high chair between our mother and me. Julie opened her mouth. June Spoon spooned in a glob of applesauce and my sister rolled the glob around in her mouth before spitting it out on the built-in tray.

"Oh, no, Julie," my mother moaned.

Barry wolfed down his chop and shoveled in rice. "Met this neat guy today," he said, talking with his mouth full. "Name's Chuck Marsland."

"Marsland?" asked our father.

"Yeah."

"I know a Mister Marsland who's an attorney. I'll bet that's his son."

I toyed with my peas. "What's so neat about Chuck?"

"He loves to fight," my brother replied.

"No fighting at Punahou," Dadio scolded. "They might expel you."

"I won't," Barry grumbled.

Chuck Marsland was a wise guy whose father served as prosecuting attorney for the State of Hawaii. He was a tall, freckle-faced kid with a mean grin. He'd been forced to repeat like Barry and saw my brother as a kindred spirit. There was a privileged air in the way he carried himself, as if he were immune to getting into trouble. His cocky stride dared even the jocks to challenge his rule over the junior high turf of Bishop Hall, Middle Field, and Castle Hall. Chuck was bigger than most 8th graders. He'd told Barry a local guy stole his surfboard at San Souci Beach and that his father tracked down the thief and beat him to a pulp. "My old man pinned the *kanak* down and let me get in a few choice punches," Chuck had bragged.

Chuck discovered I was Barry's kid brother during lunch. We all ate at Dole Cafeteria, a sprawling mess hall serving 3rd through 8th graders. You paid for lunch because Punahou was private. Rows of overhead fluorescent bulbs lighted the cafeteria and it was screened-in to discourage flies. 7th and 8th graders congregated on the Pearl Harbor side as if proximity to the start of the lunch line demonstrated seniority. 3rd graders ate on the Diamond Head side. The middle zone was where everyone else congregated although the kids got bigger moving north over the sandstone linoleum. The cafeteria buzzed with adolescent chatter. The kitchen pumped out local favorites, everything from chicken and long rice to laulau with poi to greasy slabs of Spam. Cleanup crews mopped every morning with Pine-Sol even though the smell of sour milk still lingered. Main courses were housed in stainless steel containers. A battalion of Asian women in white aprons kept us moving along and slopped food onto our plates with giant steel spoons. I could see resentment in their eyes as if we were the spawn of the privileged haole minority. Dole Cafeteria also offered American standards like hotdogs, French fries, blueberry pie, pudding, plates of quivering Jell-O, fruit cups, salads, shakes, and ice cream sundaes.

Chuck and Barry hung out on the Pearl Harbor side, five tables away from me. I sat alone. It was hard making friends at Punahou, especially since the regulars treated newcomers like outsiders with communicable diseases. Most of the new students seemed too alienated to make friends with fellow new arrivals. Chuck gestured wildly. Barry giggled his approval while chewing gum. Chuck bombed me with a pineapple wedge that skidded harmlessly across the table. A second followed, flew over my shoulder. A third came straight at me—I tried ducking but the wedge whacked my forehead.

"Direct hit!" Chuck clapped.

I retreated to the Diamond Head side, finishing my teriyaki chicken and rice in the midst of 3rd graders. I felt like a baby. Barry handed Chuck his apple. The apple sailed over me and struck a girl in the chest. She started to cry. A haole man with a tie crossed his arms and asked who'd done it. Nobody answered. He gave me the stink eye. It was as if, since I was the oldest, that made me the guilty party.

I returned my tray, hesitating at the confection bar before buying a chocolate shake. I snuck over to the Pearl Harbor side. Chuck was gabbing like a mynah bird when I dumped the shake on his head.

"Fuck!" he said.

He stood up. Chocolate cascaded down his neck, splattering his shirt and pants. The students roared. I darted for the screen door, swung it open, and ran for my life. I sprinted across Middle Field, angling for the lily pond. I was sure I could lose them because two chasers seldom run fast together. I heard heavy breathing and looked back—Chuck was right behind me. I veered toward Thurston Chapel, cut left, and lost him. But he recovered, gained ground fast, and trapped me beside the lily pond. He spun me around and got me from behind in a bear hug. Barry caught up.

"I'll tell," I gasped, "I'll tell my father."

"What'll he do?" Chuck asked.

"Sue you."

"My father'll sue 'im back."

I squirmed trying to get away but Chuck kept my arms pinned against my sides. He was stronger than my brother.

"What should we do to the little prick?" Chuck asked.

Barry stared at me. "He gets what he gets."

"See," Chuck said, squeezing. "Even your own brother hates you."

"Does not."

"You hate 'im, right?" Chuck asked.

My brother spit out his gum.

Chuck winced. "Barry?"

"I hate him."

Two haole teachers in muumuus walked up. "Boys," said one of the teachers, "what's going on here?"

"Sorry, ma'am," Chuck answered, "we're only playing."

"Well, don't play so rough."

"We won't," Chuck promised.

The teachers walked off and headed for the cafeteria.

Chuck rubbed chocolate from his hair into mine. "Want your brother dead?" he asked Barry.

"Dead as a doornail."

"Can't believe we're in the same grade, Squirt," Chuck muttered. He grabbed me and swung my legs over the water. "Dunk-a-roo time."

"No!"

He dropped me in the lily pond. I slipped on the bottom, belly-flopping on a cluster of lily pads. A frog croaked. I tried standing but the bottom was slick with algae and fell again. Pollywogs swam by.

"Surf's up, Squirt," Chuck laughed.

I watched them march arm-and-arm toward Bishop Hall. My brother was a traitor for ganging up on me. But this was nothing out of the ordinary. He was the same boy who'd paid Kahala kids 50¢-a-week not to be my friend, and joined in when a bully started pelting me with gravel after Little League.

A black cross hung on the white exterior wall of Thurston Chapel. I wanted the cross to be gold instead of black. The pond water had a greenish tint. Lily pads resembling hearts crowded the surface. I knew, deep down, I shouldn't blame my brother for distancing himself. Barry ached to fit in a class he was forced to repeat. His worst nightmare was that I'd become our father's favorite by getting better grades. He was hedging his bets by hanging out with Chuck. Even though he might not be able to compete with me academically, he knew he could beat me by being more popular.

Barry didn't have to worry about my relationship with our father being special. Whenever I did something to please him, it wouldn't be long before I slipped up and displeased him twice as much. Dadio called me "Kapahulu Hog" after catching me pigging out on Cheetos. He reprimanded me for not changing Julie's diaper before a rash set in. He scolded me for not cooking his steak medium on the hibachi. I would gaze down the hall: if my father were coming, I'd duck back inside my room. I'd quit asking for his help in math because he referred to me as "the Stupe of Honolulu." I'd confessed to stumbling on division problems in Mr. Scott's class, and proved my weakness by receiving a "C" in Mathematics. On Saturday, Dadio gave me pages of long division scrawled on a legal pad and exiled me to the table out on the lanai. The problems were scrawled in pencil and I could tell he was pissed off because the numbers were black from pressing down hard.

"I'll miss *Milton the Monster*," I groaned.

"Grow up," my father barked, "this is your future." He hustled over to a spot outside the master bedroom and poured DDT from a can into a trench. The stink drifted onto the lanai. Dadio liked being productive whenever June Spoon was out shopping, almost as if he were competing with her to see who could complete the most chores on his day off.

The stench of poison made my eyes water. I bit a fingernail staring at the first problem and wiped away a tear. I wasn't alone on the lanai. Julie was entertaining herself in the playpen while our mother was at Star Market. I liked hearing her dolls grumble and the toys squeak. A series of squeaks sounded like farts. I chuckled. I gazed over at the playpen. The DDT didn't seem to affect my sister. She sat with her back against the bars clutching a doll with a red dress.

"Kir-bee," Julie smiled at me, "my Kir-bee da bess."

Attending Punahou didn't make me swell with pride. On the contrary, it made me feel like a stranger exiled on foreign shores. Most of the boys were taller, smarter, and better looking. I seemed small, common, and insignificant in this new land. The nickname "Peanut" that my grandmother had coined fit. Something tore at my guts as I searched for identity. Who was I? Where did I fit in? Who would care if I died? I felt unloved both at home and at school. Sometimes it felt as though the only friends I had were the pet caterpillars I'd smuggled over from Moloka'i.

Making friends at my new school was difficult. Popularity and social clout were measured by hip clothes, your clique, and throwing "righteous parties." I felt like a zero moving past the inner circles of cool kids. I thought of myself as a sort of bumbling underdog like the pooch in *The Underdog Show*. But I wasn't even an underdog since I was on the periphery of the social structure. Even the cartoon dog had Polly around to rescue. I had nobody. Most boys wanted a pal they could share girl lust with, a chum who'd commiserate over dumb classes, dorky teachers, and a streak of bad grades. I was so overwhelmed with day-to-day survival that I rarely thought about making friends. Entering a clique was impossible. I understood neither hip surfer speak nor the *pakalolo* ramblings of the druggies. I despised the jocks because most were quick to make fun of the less popular. Some of the jocks tortured teachers like Mrs. Henderson: they tied the cords of her window blinds to chairs and hung the chairs out of her homeroom windows.

The Punahou girls made me swoon, mostly because they didn't wear the blue paisley skirts and white blouse uniforms of the girls at Star of the Sea. Most strutted flirtatiously around campus in mini-skirts or skintight jeans. They were a battalion of foxes that crossed Middle Field like runway models and even dared to tease the men teachers.

The 7th grade girl cheerleaders were la crème de la crème. They twirled their buff'n'blue skirts from Castle Hall to Bishop Hall before the big game on Fridays and performed synchronized dance steps on Lower Field. Sometimes they graced us with school spirit on special event days, such as Statehood Day and Halloween. The one upside to me being invisible was eavesdropping on cheerleader conversations during Study Hall. I heard sex-laced laments and confessions, everything from admissions to "going all the way" to getting dumped by players on the varsity team.

I doubted I'd ever fit into the social machinery at Punahou. Barry had already expanded his circle of friends to include a few jocks, such as Doug Scott and Pierre Pang. I joined the Science Club out of sheer desperation but felt awkward around eggheads more interested in

Einstein's equations than contemplating the wonders of the universe. I wasn't a brain. I was lousy at sports. I hated drugs and surfing. I could write but a writing club didn't exist; even if it did, I considered writing a solitary endeavor. The only class I liked was English with Mr. Gaines. He had us write stories. Putting words on paper gave me a reason to be and I worked hard on assignments. A girl named Laura Kwon said she dug my story *Pygmalion*, after Mr. Gaines tacked it to the corkboard in class. It was about a boy pigeon named Pygmalion that wanted to sing as melodious as a lyrebird to woo Florence the Sparrow away from a belligerent mynah. Pygmalion learned to sing by parroting an opera star bellowing in the shower under Pygmalion's rooftop perch. After months of struggle, Pygmalion learned to sing like a champ and won Florence's heart.

I realized Punahou was expensive and I felt guilty wanting out. That first semester was as excruciating as nails clawing a chalkboard. Fortunately, a girl offered a ray of hope. Debbie Curley was in my homeroom. Her dirty blonde hair was cropped and her long neck looked like a swan's. I liked how the morning light ignited the blonde hairs on her arms and legs. Her skirts always challenged the hem length rule established by Principal Johnson and her heels made her tower over most of the other girls. Her smile revealed a retainer but her dental gear didn't prevent her from smiling big and flashing her teeth. When it was time to pose for the homeroom picture, the photographer divided our class into small groups and had us pose for skits with funny captions.

"Read those by tomorrow," Mrs. Creele said in my skit with Debbie as we stood beside her, clutching our stacks of books. It had been great fun. Debbie found a sacred place inside of me, a realm linking angels to physical longings. I imagined her as my wife and living with her in a mansion overlooking Black Point. We took our kids to Disneyland every summer and went on junkets to Paris. Debbie was my salvation. She held the key that unlocked the door to my adolescent happiness, an ideal present buoyed up by a devotion bordering worship. I wanted to kiss her ferociously, as if our last days on earth were upon us. I ached to tell her I was in love and wanted to go steady. But I lacked the courage to confess my feelings. It felt as though I was made of straw, a boy born without a backbone whose desires would blow away in the first stiff wind. What if Debbie rejected me? Suffering her rejection would destroy me. "Play it safe," I told myself, "what will be, will be." I placed my destiny in the hands of Fate. I prayed for divine intervention, for God to steer Debbie Curley into my arms. I spotted her near the dance floor during canteen while the band played "Purple Haze." I slunk away to the gym without asking her to dance. Our first dance was at Jeff Lee's party on Diamond Head Road, a bash Jeff had invited my brother to but not me. Barry had reluctantly let me tag along. It seemed like only seconds rocking out with Debbie barefoot on the living room carpet and I could tell I was more an amusement than a love interest by the distance she kept. I asked if she wanted punch. Debbie shook her head and her blonde bangs flew out like wings. It was agony watching her dance with Jeff and then Barry. I didn't speak to Debbie the rest of the evening, choosing instead to camp on an overstuffed couch and stare out the window at the Diamond Head Lighthouse.

With the exception of Debbie Curley, junior high was a cold and alien place. It was made colder and more alien by Barry, bullies, and impenetrable cliques. The grounds were war zones mined with explosives whenever I crossed paths with Chuck Marsland, especially if he was chumming around with my brother. There were other boys I dodged, such as thugs who demanded lunch money and jocks who teased invisible types like me whenever we walked by their benches. I felt dead inside. I excelled at nothing, existing in a limbo world of mediocrity and confusion. But writing stories helped me peel back the real world of junior high like a label, where I found secrets lurking below. I'd discovered the horror of unrequited love and the double agony of being an outsider and alone. But I also considered the possibility that even the popular kids harbored insecurities in the false bravado of their inner circles.

My understanding of loneliness made me weep. The girl I loved barely knew I existed. But that understanding triggered something strange. I was in my bed, watching dusk settle in, when a beam of yellow light illuminated my window. Loneliness began nurturing my hidden side, the part that knew words had the power to capture what it meant to feel. Feelings were everything because they made me human and alive. I knew, as long as I could write how and what I felt, part of me still loved who I was. It felt safe to enter the future with a measure of hope. Hope galvanized my spirit and gave me a reason to live. Yes, it was still cloudy enough to dull the world to black and white. But now a bolt of golden light had burned through the muck of junior high and high school was only a breath away.

Notes:
haole: white
hapa haole: part Hawaiian and part white
kanak: derogatory term for a Hawaiian man
mahu: gay
makai: ocean side
pakalolo: marijuana

In Light Does She Bathe Me

Matthew Woodman

the space   She enters   Her eyes a forest
turning   Her mouth a fox threading   Her cheekbones a cloud banking   Her hands a finch
skimming   Her fingers a tendril spring-
ing   Her wrists a wild grape climbing   Her arms
a willow swaying   Her breasts a brushfire
falling   Her neck a river coursing   Her
stomach a shoreline crashing   Her feet a
current skipping   Her toes a bramble ripe-
ning   Her calves two salmon leaping   Her knees
two peaks ringing   Her thighs a canyon chan-
neling   Her hips two boulders tumbling   Her
sex a hive thrumming   Her laugh a thunder-
cloud showering   Her cry a winter blanket-
ing   Her shadow lights the space   She exits

Vegetarian Chinese

Cara Spangler

We knew something wasn't quite right the moment the tiny bell above the door tinkled at Henry's Vegetarian Chinese Cuisine on that otherwise unremarkable Friday night in Fairbanks. Not because two broad-chested men swaddled in leather appeared next to the "Please Seat Yourself" sign with guns snuggled in their waistbands. Or that when the restaurant's owner and cook, Henry Rubenstein, saw the men from behind the metal cook's partition, he pulled the droopy white hat off his head with a fist and suddenly disappeared into the kitchen, a gob of spit stretched between his guilty, open lips. The reason we paused, with chopsticks tilted between our fingers and noodles mid-suck, was because these two melon-chested men wearing sunglasses after dusk were the only people, perhaps ever, to enter Henry's Vegetarian Chinese food restaurant that were actually Chinese.

Two summers before that night, forty-year-old Henry Rubenstein moved to Fairbanks, Alaska with his wife, Gloria, and their newborn baby. Because the baby was only ever seen dressed in a knitted hat with frog eyes poking from the top and an orange and pink striped onesie, and had the perplexingly gender-neutral name of Janu, we were never able to decipher whether it was a girl or a boy and were too embarrassed to ask. Henry and Gloria were a strain of hippie largely foreign to Fairbanks. Before that, they spent the past two years living and teaching in South Korea, and before that, they studied in Vermont.

Five different sized wind chimes with various empty tones hung around the exterior of their house, a little ramshackle cottage near the reindeer farm out by the train tracks. They wore earthy-colored clothes made of felt and hemp and never used umbrellas or seemed like they were in a hurry to get anywhere. They sprinkled little nuts and seeds on all of the food they brought to the potlucks and barbecues we organized to try to get to know them better, and on weekend mornings, they reclined on their front lawn drinking dandelion tea, greeting us with an excessive friendliness we never felt we could properly match.

Sandy, the fifty-year-old retired model that lived next door to the Rubensteins, told us at our neighborhood coffee shop, North Star Java, "Sometimes Henry spends whole Saturdays putting up their hammock in different parts of the backyard. He rocks in it for an hour or so, kinda testing the air with a real critical look in his eye, and then moves it to another part of the yard and does the whole thing over again. It seems like some obsessive hammock feng shui, but I think it's nice."

Todd, the owner of the gourmet hotdog stand said, "They come in a lot. Nice people. The only customers who ever order the tofu dogs. Take the sauerkraut right off the dog and put it in their little kid's mouth. He eats that stuff right up."

Gloria Rubenstein stood five feet tall, her body dominated by take-charge hips and shoulders. Her face glowed like a ripe nectarine and we often saw her reaching through the slats of fences with safety scissors, cutting leaves and flowers from our bushy, untended gardens with an innocent smile. Henry, only a couple inches taller than Gloria, with sawdust-colored curls, took care of Janu during the day. The two were spotted at various antique stores around town in the couple of weeks between sun and snow, Henry pointing into glass cabinets and marveling at ancient Chinese sugar bowls. Janu shrieked, heels kicking the seat of the stroller, causing Mr. Dilinger behind the counter to look up from his newspaper and glare.

An old friend of theirs from the University of Alaska invited Gloria, a naturopath, to work and teach in Fairbanks. "A good reason to leave Korea," they said when we asked why they moved. They would look down at Janu then, each with one hand on the stroller and the other wrapped around each other. We wanted to hate them a little then, for their effortless happiness we couldn't begin to fathom, but instead, we felt awe.

It was a curiosity we, the neighborhood, harvested while in line at the pharmacy, getting our cars washed at the school fundraiser, stalling to talk to each other beneath street lamps during midnight dog walks. The Rubensteins seemed so consistently elated, so distressingly enthusiastic about everything: local grocery stores, the changing seasons, their soppy coleslaw meals at the salmon bake because they were strict vegetarians. They never griped or used a begrudging tone, even when talking about their wet feet or a bout of the flu that had them all in a pile on the couch, and in turn, we felt obliged to spin the same injustices we used to take so personally. Sometimes, while having coffee in the privacy of each other's living rooms, we accused the Rubensteins of inauthenticity. But when we returned to our own dirty kitchens, our hands heavy with keys and yesterday's junk mail, we discerned a sinking, tumor-like jealousy. We asked ourselves every time we picked up a Styrofoam tray of meat in the grocery store and then carefully set it back: what did the Rubensteins know that we didn't?

The winter was long that year, but it always was in Fairbanks. So long that no one ever defined the three other blurry seasons as anything but a lack of winter. We hardly noticed the Rubenstein's absence from the neighborhood at first. And if we did, we weren't too surprised. The first winter in Fairbanks was the hardest, everyone claimed, the biggest test in the move to Alaska. Some people moved away after their first winter in Fairbanks, anywhere south, never outright admitting what all those hours of darkness did to a person. But we all knew. How it turned us inward toward our own separate husks of loneliness. How the gasp of our heaters became the forehead-kiss of sounds, the first thing we woke to each morning and the last thing we heard before we fell asleep. How, even when we found ourselves in each other's dark living rooms, staring through walls of some steaming drink, we could still barely recognize each other.

But we always made a point to emerge on that first day of broad sunlight, always sometime in the beginning of March, when we collected on the street corners in puddles of melting snow. It was then when we started to ask each other about the Rubensteins. If anyone had seen them or knew how they were doing. Sandy said she had seen Henry cross their snowy yard in a bathrobe to empty the compost, but nothing else. The hammock in their backyard hadn't been taken down and now carried a lap of snow. It wasn't until a couple weeks later when the obituary appeared in the paper:

Janu Rubenstein, 6 months old, died peacefully in his crib on February 26th. Taken much too soon, he will be missed terribly by his parents, Gloria and Henry.

It was a tradition in Fairbanks amongst the neighborhood to mourn by making stew, though none of us had even heard of Sudden Infant Death Syndrome. Before we could even Google how to make stew tasty without meat, the Rubensteins started showing up everywhere around town. Randy, the flamboyant martial arts teacher, said they registered for his spring classes, sitting on the wooden floor the first day with legs bent beneath them and identical, obedient smiles. They knocked on our doors on Sunday mornings when we were still in our bathrobes and handed us zucchini bread, almost apologizing for their absence in the neighborhood. When we tried to invite them in, to offer condolences for their loss, they said, "That's very sweet of you, but we have lots to do today," and kept smiling all the way down our driveways, arms linked like French schoolgirls in the movies.

"Should we do something?" we asked each other in corners of PTA meetings. "At least send something—a card? Flowers?"

"No," we responded, almost too quickly. We wanted to believe their positive spirits were impenetrable. That grief had cycled through their perfect, self-cleansing bodies and their carefree lives would resume now that the poison of death had been flushed out. "Best not to bring it up unless they do."

When Henry bought the space on the corner of Main and Holly, the former dollar store, and announced his decision to open up the Chinese restaurant, we thought, "Good! They're moving forward! They're fighters, the Rubensteins. Not even winter and death can bring them down." And the first night the restaurant opened, six months later, we stampeded the place, making audible moans of delight to each other as if we were all crowded into a steaming Jacuzzi instead of stabbing cubes of tofu and thinking, but never saying out loud, that it tasted like absolutely nothing.

In the following months, unusual things started to happen with the Rubensteins.

Little clues we collected, but couldn't quite fit together.

It started when we ran into Hank the taxi driver at the Nanooks basketball game: "Yeah, I saw the Rubensteins. I picked them up from their house around 5 a.m. a couple weeks ago, I think. They had one big suitcase and said they were going to the airport. 'You folks going on vacation?' I asked. And Henry said something like 'not exactly.' He was sittin' in the front seat next to me, lookin' kinda washed out. I noticed they had their passports so I asked, 'Where're you off to?' I didn't think it was that personal of a question, more like small talk, but they looked sorta shifty at each other. Gloria said, 'China,' and then they both smiled real proudly at me. 'Gee, all the way to China,' I said. 'What're you doing there?' Then they got quiet. They just smiled like that all the way to the airport."

Margot, the psychic who also worked the late shift at the corner store mentioned something to us after the Sweating Honey concert: "I would see him once a week at the store, and he always had a good energy about him. He usually just bought little things, cans of soup, toilet paper, cough drops, you know, normal things. One night Henry came in around 10 p.m., whistling and swinging his key ring around, happy as usual. He bought a jar of pimento olives and told me he and Gloria were making martinis when he came to the counter. But then he threw down one more thing. And I just stopped. Do you know what he was buying? Baby bottle tops—those rubber nipples you have to replace every month or so because it collects bacteria that's bad for the baby. I looked at him weird, I couldn't help it, but he was still talking about martinis. I asked him if he wanted to come into my studio for a session. I can't do psychic readings when I don't have my crystals.

"And he said, 'Now that's an idea,' in a completely sincere, genuine sorta way, and kinda nodded his head at me. And then he left."

We were all drinking beer at the Fairbanks Police Department's annual square dance fundraiser. Frank, the one security guard at Fairbanks Bank who's worked there for 30 years, also said something strange: "Henry came to the bank every single day for three weeks, give or take. I thought, hey, it's none of my business. There are tons of reasons for bank issues. Moving back and forth between countries, for one thing. And starting a restaurant, what a nightmare. Henry always said 'Howdy Frank!' on his way in. Such a friendly guy. I never knew what he was doing there though. You can't ask questions at a bank. Money is a private thing, you know. But when he left, he never said a thing. I always smiled, tried to make eye contact with him, but he always looked all dreamy. But not a good dream. More like a nightmare."

The two bulky men took their time walking to the back of the restaurant that Friday night, disrupting the smell of grilled tofu and string beans with currents of cigar smoke, hair gel, and something else no one could agree on but everyone claimed it outweighed the others. "Liquor," Ms. Berth the principal of the elementary school said. "Naw, pussy," said Torque, the tattoo artist. "Money," Simon, the Segway tour guide said, and the rest of us nodded.

But these were all guesses pulled from fuzzy recollections, as we had already moved on to spooning up our brown rice and spilling green tea on the tablecloths. "Who were they?" we asked at the time. "Business men?" we guessed.

Only Miriam, the college girl Henry had hired as a waitress, heard the sound of clattering metal bowls and Henry's desperate voice from the storage room:

"This is just a misunderstanding, just hold on for one second—don't touch me! I can get you the money ... I'll do anything. Stop pointing that at me! It's not what it seems. Hey! Will you just listen to me?"

Miriam heard the back door slam, and when she went out, Henry had disappeared.

She told herself it was probably nothing, that Henry often went out to do errands, and returned to the restaurant where we were waiting to be served.

High school juniors, Toby and Rachel, were making out in the back of Rachel's truck when they saw the black Escalade pull up in front of the Rubenstein's house. One of the men got out of the driver's seat and opened the back door where Henry stumbled to the pavement, pushed out by the other man.

"Stop! You can't do this! She's ours now, you hear me? We love her, we take care of her, she's ours," he kept crying. "She's ours!"

Cara Spangler

Gloria came out of the house in a white bathrobe then, panic on her glowing face like a tortured Buddha. The two men pulled Henry up by either arm and led him to the little wooden house, the wind chimes silent for once.

"Gloria! Lock the door, go inside, now!" Henry yelled, warbled and high-pitched like an opera singer. But one of the men reached the door before her and disappeared inside, Gloria's voice awakening with a scream. A moment later the man came out, sunglasses aglow with the reflection of a pink blanket tucked around a little face. A sleeping Chinese baby girl.

Gloria grabbed at the man's elbows, hitting his leather coat with helpless fists.

Henry flew to Gloria, as the two men walked stonily back to the car, opening the trunk to reveal a pale baby carrier amidst stacks of cardboard boxes.

"We can't, we can't, sweetie, we can't do anything about it now," Henry yelled, anger fading from his voice. As the Escalade paused at the stop sign at the end of the street and Henry and Gloria wailed into each other's hollow shoulders, the wind chimes roused themselves into a bitter cacophony.

It all happened so fast, we were still waiting for our fortune cookies when someone rushed in and told us. No one got up. No one even looked curiously at each other. It was as if we could all communicate by staring through our little portions of muddled soup. We recognized the clues then, wondered how we hadn't seen them sooner. We grieved for the Rubensteins. For the stolen baby we would never meet, the phony adoption papers, the illegal secret they couldn't afford. But we also grieved for ourselves. For believing in the invincibility of the Rubensteins, needing it as a sort of beacon. Looking down at our spilled noodles, our greasy napkins, we were suddenly hyper-aware of our own failing efforts toward that sort of seemingly easy happiness, a shadow of the ever-impending winter here, even in the midst of summer. Even though we didn't yet know about the immediate closure of the restaurant, the move to Nepal, the eventual divorce—we all agreed then—we had to let the Rubensteins go.

Contributors

Tricia Cantillon is a native Californian. After receiving her BA in Creative Writing, she began writing both fiction and non-fiction. She currently lives in Los Angeles with her husband and two children. Previous work has been published in *The Berkeley Fiction Review*.

J.L. Cooper is a writer and psychologist in Sacramento, California. His work explores the lyrical voice and the pursuit of imagery in the telling of a life. Awards include first place in Short Short Story, 2013, in *New Millennium Writings*, and second place in Essay, 2014, in *Literal Latte*. His work has appeared or is forthcoming in *Oberon Poetry Journal*, *The Manhattan Review*, *Gold Man Review*, *Subliminal Interiors*, *Flutter Poetry Journal*, *The Sun* (Reader's Write), *Kind of a Hurricane Press*, and *KY Story* (anthology).

Jessica Danger lives in Southern California where she teaches creative writing and composition in classrooms and libraries ranging from elementary school to college to adults in evening school. Her short stories have been published in *Wild Quarterly* and *Crux Literary Journal*. She is a masters of fine arts candidate at Bennington College. She will forever defend the Oxford Comma.

Elizabeth DeBunce is a writer from Southern Oregon who is currently majoring in English and Classical Studies at Lewis & Clark College. She spends most of her free time knitting, listening to *The Mountain Goats*, and sitting with her cats through thunder storms. She most enjoys writing about eggs, whether metaphorically or not; sadly, no egg poems are included here.

Graham Guest has published work in fiction, creative non-fiction, philosophy, and music (band - Moses Guest). Graham teaches in the English Department at Dominican University of California and lives with his wife and daughter in Mill Valley, CA.

When people learn Pamela Hanson spent over thirty years in San Diego, their response is, "What? Why would you move?" Her response: "Portland offers a perfect combination of city life with a small town feel." Pamela's writing career started with a self-published novel. *The Ecliptic Principle* is her first short story. She is currently working on a poetry collection about women in relationships with non-committal men. Swimming and yoga help her relax and recharge.

Melissa Hedges is a graduate of Stephen F. Austin State University, where she studied creative writing. After residing in Hawaii for almost a year, island life has helped her "chill out" (just a bit) and sent her tastebuds into a tizzy with malasadas and plate lunches. Currently, she works hard at her day job to support her state sponsored addiction to beach drinks with tiny umbrellas.

Kelsey Hunkins has been published in the *Suisun Valley Review* for her prose fiction pieces "How to Lose your Virginity: A Ladies' Guide" and "Baby I did it for you." She plans to continue with her creative writing and hopefully do some story boarding for video games as a career.

Sarah Isto lives on the coast in Juneau, but spends March and September in the interior of Alaska at a cabin in the Kantishna Hills—no road, telephone, electricity, or internet, but lots of outdoor time and writing time. She is the author of two non-fiction books published by the University of Alaska Press. Her poetry has appeared in various issues of *Cirque* and *Tidal Echoes*.

Sasha Ives grew up in rural Connecticut and began her further education at FIT in Manhattan before transferring to Willamette University in Salem, Oregon to pursue her degree in English/Creative Writing and French Studies. Although she rests at the cusp of beginning the first stage of her career with Nordstrom, she continues to harbor the dream of writing novels atop a mountain in the south of France.

Kelsey Lahr has worked summers as a park ranger in Yosemite National Park since 2008. She holds a BA in Communication Studies from Westmont College in Santa Barbara, CA, and is currently pursuing a Master's in Communication at the University of Utah. Her research focuses on organizational discourse and employee wellbeing in environmental organizations. Her essays about life in Yosemite have appeared in *The Copperfield Review* and *Dark Matter*.

Charlene Langur is a southern Californian, an organic gardener, and a Syracuse University Graduate Writing Fellow. Her writing has appeared in *The Stone Canoe*, *The Hampden Sydney Poetry Review*, *The Adirondack Review*, most currently in *Blueline*, *Cold Mountain Review*, *Pamplemousse*, *Earth's Daughters*, forthcoming poems in *Spoon River Poetry Anthology* and *The Buddhist Poetry Review*, a series of poems in

Poetry East as well as in *Weber—The Contemporary West* in Fall of 2015.

Amanda Lara resides in Orange County, California. Prior to her work in creative writing, she wrote a bimonthly column for her city newspaper, the *Fullerton Observer*. Her latest piece of published fiction was featured in the YA magazine *Inaccurate Realities*. She can be found on both Instagram and Twitter @missamandalara.

Mercedes Lawry has published poetry in such journals as *Poetry, Nimrod, Prairie Schooner, Poetry East, Natural Bridge*, and others. Thrice-nominated for a Pushcart Prize, she's published two chapbooks, most recently "Happy Darkness". She's also published short fiction, essays and stories and poems for children. She lives in Seattle.

Born and raised in Glasgow, Scotland, Iain Macdonald currently lives in Arcata, California. He has earned his bread and beer in various ways, from flower picker to factory hand, merchant marine officer to high school teacher. His chapbooks, *Plotting the Course* and *Transit Report*, are published by March Street Press. A third chapbook, *The Wrecker's Yard*, has been accepted for publication by Kattywompus Press.

Sandra McDow is an Oregon writer who splits her time between Oregon's mid-Willamette Valley, and the Oregon coast. She primarily writes short fiction, but is currently undertaking her first novel. Sandra is a student in the Northwest Institute of Literary Arts' MFA program. She belongs to two critique groups, Willamette Writers Association, and the Pacific Northwest Writers Association. Sandra's has previously published in *The Riverwalk Journal*, and *Gold Man Review*.

Shaun Anthony McMichael lives in Seattle with his wife and quiet writing habit. He currently teaches ESL to immigrants and is pursuing a Masters in Teaching after many years informally educating his city's troubled youth in creative writing and other subjects. His fiction has appeared or is forthcoming in a number of literary magazines including, *Litro, Existere, The Milo Review, Night Train, Carrier Pigeon*, and *Euphony*.

Amy Miller's writing has appeared in numerous journals, including *Bellingham Review, Gold Man Review, Nimrod, Rattle, ZYZZYVA, Asimov's Science Fiction, Fine Gardening*, and *The Poet's Market*. Author of ten chapbooks, she won the Cultural Center of Cape Cod National Poetry Competition, judged by Tony Hoagland, and has been a finalist for the Pablo Neruda Prize and the 49th Parallel Award. She works as the publications manager for the Oregon Shakespeare Festival and blogs at writers-island.blogspot.com.

Nancy Carol Moody is the author of *Photograph with Girls* (Traprock Books), and her poems have appeared in *The Southern Review*, *The Los Angeles Review*, *Salamander*, *The Journal* and *Nimrod*. In addition to writing, Nancy makes collages with torn-up paper, a process not unlike the way she builds her poems. Her new manuscript is titled *The House of Nobody Home*. When she's not on a train, Nancy lives in Eugene, Oregon.

Travis Laurence Naught is an author who happens to be a quadriplegic wheelchair user. Two books of his confessional style poetry, *The Virgin Journals* (ASD Publishing, 2012) and *Still Journaling* (e-book, 2013), are widely available. Individual poems and stories by Travis have been published online (*Deadman's Reach*, *BALLOONS Lit Magazine*, et al.) and in print (*Freshwater Poetry Journal*, *Lost Coast Review*, et al.). Check out naughtapoet.blogspot.com for more original writing and information about Travis!

Jamie North has an MFA from St. Mary's College of CA. Her poems most recently appear in APIARY and VINYL. She is currently working on a chapbook *Love, Place, Soma*.

Maureen O'Leary is a writer and educator from Sacramento. She is the author of the novels *How to Be Manly*, *The Arrow*, and the forthcoming *The Ghost Daughter*. Her short stories and poetry appear in the publications of *Esopus*, *Night Train*, *Brackish Vol. 2*, *Revolution John*, *Prick of the Spindle*, *Shade Mountain Press*, and *Heyday Press*.

Daniel Pecchenino lives in Hollywood and is on the Writing Program faculty at the University of Southern California. He is the Reviews Editor at *Dialogist*, and his poetry and criticism have appeared in *The Los Angeles Review*, *Gravel*, *Two Hawks Quarterly*, *Borderlands: Texas Poetry Review*, and other publications.

B. B. Pirelli is a graduate of Willamette University. Pirelli grew up and currently resides in the San Francisco Bay Area.

Dorothy M. Place lives and writes in Davis, California. Since starting her writing career in 2006, she has published eight short stories in literary journals. They include *The Yolo Crow* (2), *Todd Point Review*, *Cha, An Asian Literary Journal*, *bioStories*, *The Flagler Review*, *Four Cham-*

bers (forthcoming), and *Gold Man Review* (forthcoming). Her story, "The Full Moon," won first prize in the Mendocino Coast Writers short story contest and the Estelle Frank Fellowship (2010).

Kori Rosset is a short story author and screenwriter. She has had short stories published and anthologized in *Labyrinth Literary Journal*, and others. When she isn't busy writing or thrashing gender norms, she's probably playing music or thinking too much.

Gerard Sarnat has been published in about a hundred poetry journals and has authored critically-acclaimed 2010's HOMELESS CHRONI-CLES from Abraham to Burning Man, 2012's Disputes, and 2014's 17s. He's a physician who's setup and staffed clinics for the disenfranchised, a CEO of healthcare organizations, and a Stanford professor. For *Huffington Post* reviews, reading dates including Stanford and more; visit GerardSarnat.com.

Jeremy Schnee received his MFA from Colorado State University. His stories have been published in *New Plains Review*, *Exit 7*, and *Dark Corners*. He lives in Portland, Oregon and is working on his first novel. For more information about his writing, please visit www.jeremyschnee.com.

Patty Somlo's essay, "If We Took a Deep Breath," which appeared in the *Gold Man Review*, was selected as a Notable Essay of 2013 for *Best American Essays 2014*. She has received four Pushcart Prize nominations and one for storySouth's Million Writers Award. Author of *From Here to There and Other Stories*, Somlo's second book, *Hairway to Heaven Stories*, is forthcoming in January 2017 from Cherry Castle Publishing.

Cara Spangler is pro-snack but anti-pretentious food mashup. She has a degree in writing from the University of Victoria and is an editor for a progressive online community called *Care2*. Currently this burrito snob lives in Oakland, CA and runs up mountains at granny-pace for fun.

Terry Spohn has an MFA from the University of Iowa. His short stories, prose poems and poetry have appeared in *Rattle, The Sow' s Ear Poetry Review, The North American Review, Mississippi Review, Ascent, Grub Street, Oyster Boy Review, Up the Staircase, Eclectica, Mobius: the Magazine of Social Change*, and other places, including numerous anthologies. He lives with his wife, Dionne, in Escondido, California.
Emily Strauss has an M.A. in English, but is self-taught in poetry, which

she has written since college Over 250 of her poems appear in a wide variety of online venues and in anthologies, in the U.S. and abroad. The natural world is generally her framework; she also considers the stories of people and places around her and personal histories. She is a semi-retired teacher living in California.

Alex Vigue is a Washington State writer with a degree in creative writing from Western Washington University. Alex has been published in *Phantom Drift*, *Jeopardy's* 50th anniversary issue, and *Emerge Literary Journal* among others. He is the fiction editor for *Dirty Chai Lit Magazine* and he hopes to have a collection of his works published soon. You can find him on twitter @Kingwithnoname

Victoria Waddle has been published in *The Del Sol Review*, *Publisher's Weekly*, *Inlandia: A Literary Journey*, *Bosque Magazine*, and has been selected for publication in *The Huffington Post's* "50Fiction" contest. She periodically writes a book column for *The Press Enterprise* newspaper in California's Inland Empire. As a high school teacher librarian, she blogs about literature of interest to teens at "School Library Lady."

Thomas Walton's work has appeared in *ZYZZYVA*, *Gambling the Aisle*, *Bombay Gin*, and other journals. His work was recently anthologized in *Make It True*; *Poetry from Cascadia*. He lives in Seattle where he edits *PageBoy Magazine*.

Lillo Way's poems have appeared in *Poet Lore*, *The Madison Review*, *Santa Fe Literary Review*, *The Sow's Ear Poetry Review*, *Poetry East*, *Yemassee*, *Common Ground Review*, *Permafrost*, *Cordite Review* (Australia), *Tampa Review*, *Third Wednesday*, *Freshwater*, *Quiddity*, and *WomenArts Quarterly* among others. Her poems have been anthologized in "Weatherings" (*FutureCycle Press*) and in the bird anthology, "Poeming Pigeons." She has received grants from the NEA, NY State Council on the Arts, and the Geraldine R. Dodge Foundation for her choreographic work involving poetry. She has been a frequent reader on NPR's "Selected Shorts."

Pat Phillips West lives in Portland, OR. A Pushcart and Best of the Net nominee, her work has appeared in *Haunted Waters Press*, *Persimmon Tree*, *VoiceCatcher*, *San Pedro River Review*, *Slipstream* and elsewhere.

Matthew Woodman teaches writing at California State University, Bakersfield and has had poems appear in recent issues of *Hinchas de Poesia*, *California Journal of Poetics*, *Sierra Nevada Review*, *Santa Clara*

Review, The Timberline Review, and *Fourteen Hills.*

Kirby Wright once roamed the same Honolulu junior high as President Obama and Kelly Preston. He is the author of the companion novels PUNAHOU BLUES and MOLOKA'I NUI AHINA, both set in the islands. He will be filming the trailer for THE END, MY FRIEND, his futuristic thriller, in Hollywood this fall.